Praise for
Ethel Ray: Living in the White, Gray, and Black

"… a significant contribution to our community's understanding of what it meant to be Black in Duluth, Minnesota during the early 1900s. The story offers challenges to the reader regarding the psychological, intergenerational impacts of racism on different family members, and also new perspectives on these events through the eyes of a young woman who found her way through."

Heidi Bakk-Hansen
Co-founder, Clayton, Jackson, McGhie Memorial

"A groundbreaking bit of original research. We don't have enough of these stories. We need these little chapters of our history – family – personal episodes, which enriches the general history of peoplehood. We should be grateful to Karen F. Nance and her family tracing a legacy of Black people in the city of Duluth and greater Minnesota. Many people do not know about Black people living in Duluth let alone know about the tragedy of Elias Clayton, Elmer Jackson, and Isaac McGhie at the hands of lynchers. Kudos Karen F. Nance and other descendants of Ethel's for revealing this story.

This riveting inciteful and well written chapter in the Black American story is a great contribution to our collective history and humanity."

Mahmoud El-Kati
Professor Emeritus of History, Macalester College
Author of *The Myth of Race/The Reality of Racism*

"[This] is a very poignant, complicated, and inspiring story. It provides insight into the [lives of] Black residents of the region through pictures, narrative, and journal entries from Ethel Ray's family. Most importantly Karen Nance helps readers understand how the lynching affected this family's lives and other Black residents of Duluth, MN… I am so proud to know about the history and legacy of Ethel Ray through this book. My hope is that this book will become fuel for discussion about the history of this region."

Paula Gudmundson, Nordic Center of Duluth

"Inspiring! Fantastic! Powerful!

Thank you for letting me spend time getting to know our ancestor, Ethel Ray. This is a story that we should all get to know... The more I think I know, the more I am embarrassed by the sheroes I don't know, who have been hidden in plain sight. Ethel Ray is one of the most dynamic women of the 20th century and is a warrior. Schools need to add this book to their shelves, and this will become a book club favorite."

Ezra Hyland
University of Minnesota,
College of Education & Human Development

"Facts and personal information shared were superbly interwoven in this biography of Ethel Ray … and discriminatory challenges she faced while growing up in Minnesota. The poems included gave a superb touch to the material written. The coup de grace from start to finish is Ethel Ray morphing into a conscientious [leader] for civil rights and remaining Black!"

Craig Nance
Ethel Ray's oldest grandchild. Glenn Ray Nance's son

"Ethel Ray is an eye-opening account of a young Black girl and her family living in Duluth, Minnesota, at the turn of the 20th century. The oppressive racism of the time comes through starkly in the diaries of Ethel and her father, William Henry Ray—as does the spirit and tenacity with which they seek to rise above it. In describing the difficult choices that Ethel and her family make in grappling with ever-present discrimination, Ms. Nance captures the complex reality of the era's racial politics with discernment and skill. Ethel Ray and her father are important Duluthians; Ms. Nance gives them the platform they deserve. Duluth is richer for her work."

John Ramos
Publisher/Investigative Reporter
Duluth Monitor Newspaper

"[This book] provides a look into the life of one of Minnesota's great unsung heroes… it also gives voice to a vital narrative that is absent from our collective history. The Ethel Ray story highlights the challenges interracial families and biracial children in this country have had to face for more than a hundred years. This is a story about one woman's determination to be a change agent and stands as an example for all of us to seek true justice and embrace our shared humanity."

Susan Smith-Grier
Writer, Copywriter, Award-Winning Poet

"In an era of simplistic historical soundbites, easy labels, and stereotypes, Karen Nance's book, is a reminder of the complex reality of American history. Covering both the Ray's inner struggles with multiple self-identities to the struggle for survival amid the tragic racial violence around them, this book is a thought-provoking piece of personal and national history exploring race, culture, and humanity."

Traci Thompson, Certified Genealogist

"Ethel Ray Nance, like such Minnesota icons as Josie Johnson (Hope in the Struggle) or Alan Page (All Rise), worked to change America. Ethel Ray: Living in the White, Gray and Black now honors her memory and accomplishments with an account by granddaughter Karen Felicia Nance. It's well written, a straightforward narrative, reflecting with clarity on Nance's early life. This book's national importance is without doubt. Its significance to Minnesotans, particularly her Duluth experiences, can't be overstated."

Dwight Hobbes
Minneapolis/St. Paul Magazine, Minnesota Reformer

"Mixed with great accomplishments, such as those of Ethel Ray, are the realities of being Black in America. And yet, Ethel Ray reminds us that we have the power to choose how the traumas define us or we rise above them for the future of the next generation."

Dr. Wanda Tucker
Faculty Emeritus, Rio Salado College

Ethel Ray: Living in the White, Gray, and Black

by

Karen Felecia Nance

In Black Ink
St. Paul, Minnesota USA

© 2024 by Karen Felecia Nance

First Printing

Printed in the United States of America

All rights reserved. International copyright secured. No part of this book may be reproduced, stored in a retrieval system, or transmitted in any form or by any means, whether electronic, mechanical, photocopying, recording, or otherwise, without prior written permission of the publisher, except for inclusion of brief quotations in an acknowledged review.

Ethel Ray: Living in the White, Gray, and Black
by Karen Felecia Nance

ISBN 979-8-9895065-0-7	Softcover	Non-Redacted
ISBN 979-8-9895065-1-4	Softcover	Redacted
ISBN 979-8-9895065-2-1	Hardcover	Non-Redacted

Summary
This biography as told by Karen Felecia Nance, granddaughter of Ethel Ray Nance, provides a window into the early life of an amazing woman. Ethel Ray was an African American woman who grew up in Duluth, Minnesota, between 1889 and 1923. She and her biracial family endured the challenge in northern Minnesota of creating community and fostering a place where their family could be free.

Content Editing	Lanise "Lenny" Prater and Uri-Biia Si-Asar
Poetry	Lanise "Lenny" Prater
Copyeditor	Danielle Magnuson
Book Designer	Christopher Harrison
Cover Art	Leslie Barlow
Printer	Smith Printing Company LLC

In Black Ink
938 Selby Avenue • St. Paul, Minnesota 55104
InBlackInk.org • Info@InBlackInk.org

This book is dedicated to my great-grandfather William Henry Ray, to my grandmother Ethel Ray Nance, and to my uncle Glenn Ray Nance.

These three extraordinary souls have left an indelible mark on history and in my heart. Their lives, stories, and unwavering commitment to justice have shaped the narrative of our shared humanity.

To William Henry Ray, who died ten years before I was born, you are a beacon of strength and resilience. Your unwavering dedication to Civil Rights for Black people laid the foundation for future generations to stand tall and demand equality. Your legacy of courage continues to inspire us to challenge the status quo and fight for a more just society.

To Ethel Ray Nance, the remarkable woman for whom this book is written, your spirit burned with the fire of justice. Your unwavering pursuit of Civil Rights and your undeniable strength of character serve as a testament to the power of persistence and the transformative potential of everyone. Your remarkable commitment to the cause of equality has paved the way for progress and lit the path for those to follow.

To Glenn Ray Nance, a custodian of history and a guardian of truth, your invaluable contribution of material for this book has allowed the story of Ethel Ray—your mother, my grandmother—to be told with authenticity and depth. Through your insights and memories, you have breathed life into her journey and ensured her legacy endured.

In *Ethel Ray: Living in the White, Gray, and Black,* I honor the struggles, triumphs, and sacrifices of each of you. Through these pages, I celebrate the resilience of the human spirit and the transformative power of love, justice, and compassion.

May this book serve as a testament to your extraordinary lives and inspire generations to come to embrace the fight for equality, to challenge prejudice, and to live with unwavering dedication to justice.

With deepest admiration and gratitude,

Your legacy,

Karen Felecia Nance

Literary Consideration

This publication is a historical narrative based on actual events and actual people that took place in the United States in the late 1800s and early 1900s. This literary work tells a story reflective of the time period regarding relationships between the Black and white communities. Within this sphere, the derogatory N-word was used. In this edition of the book, the N-word is used with its full spelling. This may cause visceral responses within readers. A redacted edition is available.

Additionally, there is a photo that spans pages 52-53 of the actual lynching that occurred in Duluth, Minnesota. This image may cause visceral responses within readers. Please skip these pages if this is a concern.

Contents

Foreword
Preface

Introduction	1
1. An Immigration/Migration Story in the North Star State	3
2. The Formative Years and Young Adulthood	22
3. Lynching Is as American as Apple Pie	41
4. Severance	67
Epilogue	81
Acknowledgments	83
Appendix	85

    Timeline
    Family Tree
    The Black Population in Minnesota
    List of Images
    List of Poems
    References and Resources
    About the Author

Foreword

Ethel Ray Nance of Duluth, Minnesota, is a United States African-heritage hero. She is a Minnesota icon. She is an undisputed legend and one of the most important Minnesotans to serve the people of the United States. Every person in Duluth, and in the state of Minnesota as a whole, should know about this remarkable Minnesotan. Educating our children about Ethel Ray Nance must be a priority, and teaching opportunities must be available at every grade level across the state.

Ethel Ray Nance was born on April 13, 1899, in Duluth. She graduated from Duluth Central High School in 1917. She was sought after by numerous organizations due to her prolific and professional service as a stenographer and researcher. Ethel was one of the most important Civil Rights and women's rights advocates to come out of the state of Minnesota. She has a long and storied history in America.

The story about Ethel Ray Nance is American history at its finest. Author and attorney Karen Felecia Nance, Ethel's granddaughter, presents an important perspective about the life and legacy of her beloved family member. *Ethel Ray: Living in the White, Gray, and Black* is an important historical and educational document for all to take in and to grow from.

In 1928, Nance became the first African-heritage police officer in Minnesota's largest police department, the Minneapolis Police Department. That was during the era of lynchings in this country. To succeed as an African-heritage individual at that level, despite the difficulties of racism and sexism, is remarkable in and of itself.

That was certainly not the only accomplishment for Nance. She was a prolific writer and researcher. She worked with the National Urban League in Kansas City, Missouri, and in New York. Nance also served the NAACP and as a secretary for W. E. B. Du Bois, one of the founders of the NAACP. Her apartment in Harlem was known as the Harlem West Side Literary Salon, a gathering location for many well-known writers of the Harlem Renaissance. She too participated in the Harlem Renaissance as a writer.

Ethel Ray Nance was a bad Sista! That's s-i-s-t-a. She was a bad Sista! And that was way back in the day! Duluthians should feel proud that such a fine person as Nance called Duluth her home. Nance hailed from the Central Hillside neighborhood. This is a proud and inspiring Central Hillside fact that our African-heritage children and families can embrace. Let's continue to aspire to greatness just as Ethel Ray did. Ethel Ray also was a contributing writer to the publication *Negro History Bulletin*.

Ethel Ray Nance, the legend she has become, should serve as a reminder that American greatness has the potential to come from all of us. Aspiring to be great is in fact a game changer. Let's honor Ethel Ray Nance as a significant game changer in Minnesota and in the nation.

By reading this book about Ethel Ray Nance, we are honoring an American hero and recognizing a legend. She succeeded despite any and all obstacles put in her way. As you read this story about Ethel Ray Nance, keep in mind what the great poet Maya Angelou told us: "When you learn, teach. When you get, give." Please share this Duluth legend among your family, friends, and fellow community members. We will be richer and wiser for it.

Henry L. Banks

Duluth resident for forty years
Duluth School Board member, District 3
Developer, Senior producer, and Host of the People of Color with Henry Banks show
Founder and Emeritus Co-chair of the Clayton Jackson McGhie Memorial

Preface

When my grandmother Ethel Ray Nance was in her nineties, she gave me many letters and articles documenting her life, and I promised I would write her biography. This is not the book I intended to write. I envisioned telling the complete Ethel Ray Nance story within a single volume; however, I have come to realize several books could be written about her multidimensional life and a documentary made. I decided to focus, in this book, on her childhood and young adult days. I also realized in order to authentically tell the story of her early life, I needed to travel to Duluth, Minnesota—her birthplace. I made my first trip from my home in San Francisco to Duluth in 2021. While researching her story, I made contact with some wonderful people who shared amazing stories.

One story brought up happened when my grandmother was twenty-one years old. It involved the lynching of three Black men in Duluth. Her family lived just a few blocks away from the location of the lynching. I spoke with Michael Fedo, author of the 1979 book *The Lynchings in Duluth*, previously titled *They Was Just Niggers*, and the documentarian Daniel Oyinloye, a longtime Duluth resident, who also produced a short documentary about the lynchings. I felt inspired to add to the historical record of this unfortunate event. The lynchings no doubt reflected life as they knew it back in 1920 Duluth.

My day-to-day life took my focus off the book until my father, Thatcher Popel Nance, Ethel's son, passed away suddenly in 2013. It was good to spend time with Glenn Ray Nance, my father's brother, after the memorial service. He has always been warm, welcoming, and loving. I shared with my uncle Glenn that I wanted to focus on writing my grandmother's life story. He was supportive and graciously provided me with many additional books and papers he had in his possession belonging to Ethel and her father, William Henry Ray. Ethel's love for me was manifesting itself through my uncle. Combing through hundreds of documents provided some healing from her death and my father's death. This book, I hope, is the first of many.

My father was born Thatcher Williams in Washington, D.C. in 1933, the first son of Ethel Ray and LeRoy Alexis Herbert Williams, who had married in Anoka, Minnesota, in 1929. LeRoy and Ethel had a second son, Glenn, and lived in Minneapolis with their two boys. The couple divorced in 1943, after which Ethel and the children never had contact with LeRoy again. In 1944, Ethel remarried Clarence Aristotle Nance in Seattle. Clarence was a US Navy soldier who had fought in World War II. Since neither Thatcher nor Glenn had contact with their biological father, they changed their last names from Williams to Nance.

In May 1945, Dr. W. E. B. Du Bois wired Ethel asking her to serve as his secretary at the founding of the United Nations, where he was the consultant to the American delegation. Ethel accepted and moved her family—Clarence, Thatcher, and Glenn—to San Francisco, California, where they lived at 204 Hilltop Road in the Bayview–Hunter's Point area. From June through July of 1945, Ethel left her family to live in New York City, where she worked as W. E. B. Du Bois's research assistant at the NAACP's National Office. While in that position, Ethel set up the NAACP Regional Office in San Francisco for the purpose of directing work to that office. She accepted the full-time position of special administrator of the NAACP West Coast branches in Hawaii and Alaska. Her husband, Clarence, worked as an electrician.

I was born in San Francisco in 1958. Growing up with my father, after my parent's divorce, I was not raised with a Black identity and did not spend much time with my grandmother or uncle. I would develop this consciousness later, during my high school years when I was not living with my father. When I was fourteen years old, I moved to Berkeley, California, across the Bay, with my mother Fannie Mae Westbrooks. She influenced me with her involvement in the Black Power movement, the Poor People's Campaign, and many other Black community events in nearby Oakland, California. These activities played a significant role in my coming into consciousness as a Black woman.

Fortunately, my mother urged me to spend time with my paternal grandmother, Ethel, who still resided a short distance away in San Francisco. Ethel was a dedicated member of the California Bay Area NAACP–GI Assistance Committee, which raised more than $5,000 to support Thurgood Marshall, who was serving as special counsel for the NAACP in 1951. At this time, Marshall was investigating allegations of widespread discriminatory court martials of African American servicemen in Tokyo, Japan. Marshall was a prominent figure in the fight for equality of African Americans. His most significant victory came in 1954 when he successfully argued the landmark case of Brown v. Board of Education before the US Supreme Court. This ruling brought an end to racial segregation in public schools. Then, in 1967, Thurgood Marshall made history by becoming the first African American Supreme Court justice.

My grandmother involved me in her endeavors with the organization she co-founded, the San Francisco African American Historical & Cultural Society. She served on several boards of directors from 1974 to 1977, including the board of the African American Historical Society and the Sickle Cell Anemia Disease Research Foundation board. It was through her connections with multiple organizations that my grandmother arranged for me to attend the 1975 Hall of Fame event which was the second Oscar Micheaux Awards Ceremony in Oakland. This event promoted Black filmmaking and preserved the contributions of African American artists both in front of and behind the camera. It also sponsored advanced screening of films by and about people of African descent. Guest film stars presenting the awards that evening included James Earl Jones, Brock Peters, Brenda Sykes, Ester Rolle, and Bernie Casey.

When Alex Haley, author of the book Roots, was in San Francisco in 1977, my grandmother arranged for me to attend one of his speeches, and I was able to have him autograph my copy of his book, the summer after my college freshman year. Later that year, I participated in Operation Crossroads Africa and coincidentally was assigned to a group in Gambia, the country where Alex Haley had traced his ancestral roots. I convinced our group leader to travel to Haley's village of Juffureh, where we met the eldest living Haley ancestor. My Crossroads experience included traveling to Senegal, Mali, Burkina Faso, Ivory Coast, and Ghana.

When I returned home and shared my travel experiences with my grandmother, she never mentioned that she knew W. E. B. Du Bois or that he had asked her to move to Ghana with him and his wife in 1961. Her sole focus was me and my experiences. My grandmother was good friends with author, philosopher, theologian, educator, and Civil Rights leader Howard Thurman. She arranged for me to meet him, and he discussed his 1979 autobiography, With Head and Heart. My grandmother "hired" me to do secretarial work at the San Francisco African American Historical & Cultural Society. Unbeknownst to me, she paid my salary out of her own pocket. I vividly remember telling my grandmother I was writing a school paper about Frederick Douglass, and she pulled the 1963 Ebony magazine featuring Frederick Douglass on the cover off the shelf and said, "This may be of some assistance to you."

My grandmother's work with the NAACP—instrumental in challenging the legal systemic racism embedded in America's core institutions of education, public transportation, and public accommodation—is what made me become interested in law. When I reflect on all I have done in my life, from a young woman till now, a seasoned attorney with her own podcast and published books, I can't help but acknowledge that what my grandmother was doing all along was preparing me to become a community servant and a conscious Black woman like herself.

My grandmother lived independently in her San Francisco apartment until her early nineties, when she began having difficulty maneuvering and began falling, unable to get up without assistance. My father and uncle moved my grandmother to an assisted living center forty miles away.

This wasn't an end-of-life move for my grandmother, however. She went on to conduct several interviews, recalling more than ninety years of adventures and accomplishments. During many of my visits, she inquired about moving out, longing for privacy and family connection. Once she suggested, "Why don't you look into the two of us relocating to the YMCA?" I felt tremendous guilt not being able to move her out of there. It was disheartening not to be able to comply. She never stopped inquiring, and I never stopped searching my heart for a solution.

One day, my grandmother entrusted me with a packet of papers and asked me to "hold onto them." I felt no rush to examine these papers as there was no doubt in my mind she would live to be one hundred. God had other plans. She passed away in 1992 at the age of ninety-three.

I thought about my grandmother daily after she passed, and I finally investigated what was in the packet. This book represents only a small part of the life of Ethel Ray revealed to me from the contents of the packet, as well as other gems I ferreted out from newspaper articles, letters, interviews, photos, and keepsakes that my uncle Glenn shared.

Ethel Ray Nance is mentioned in hundreds of books, articles, and documentaries. However, to date, there is not a book solely focused on her life and contributions as a Civil Rights activist. She is more than just a footnote or a one-liner in a publication. In this book, based on Ethel's early and young adult life in Duluth, you will feel her young fighting spirit grow and her mind come into consciousness as her father guides and teaches her about living in the white, gray, and black of America.

Introduction

"The only Black people in Minnesota is Prince and Kirby Puckett."
—Chris Rock

There is a standing disbelief that Black people would settle in the Midwest, and I don't think this assumption is ridiculous. I can't deny there was a time when Black Minnesotans lay wearily in silence in fear of drowning in a sea of whiteness. Being in the North didn't mean the instinct to survive dwindled. In the early 1900s, in the remote northern city of Duluth, Minnesota, it was hard for Black Minnesotans to keep their heads above water. My grandmother Ethel Ray and her family found themselves victims of violence in both active and passive forms, and they lived through an incredibly frightening mob lynching. The hatred felt by the white residents of Duluth crashed like waves and sparked a race riot, and their rope found three Black necks to break the silence. Black and biracial families shook in rhythm to the sound of swinging ropes, which stretched like twine holding an overbearing weight until they couldn't handle the snap. This separation presented itself in the families capable of dancing between the racial divide. The unions of whites and Blacks created children who squirmed in the awkward gray area and struggled to communicate that none of them felt completely satisfied nor safe, so they settled into whatever felt the most sane. For my grandmother Ethel Ray, her parents, and her siblings, that meant a host of things—which manifested in their aspiring for the white, existing in the gray, and living in the black.

Ethel Ray was born in Duluth in 1899 and died in Alameda, California, in 1992. She was the daughter of a Black man from North Carolina and a white Swedish immigrant. Ethel had her grandchildren call her Mormor, the Swedish word for "mother of mother" or grandmother. She had never learned the language herself. Although she never said it, I thought it was Ethel's way to honor and share Great-grandmother Inga with us.

    Ethel Ray was a woman of many worlds. She was born in a gray area that could be all consuming, but Ethel didn't see it as that herself. Even living in between the realities of what came with whiteness and Blackness in American society, Ethel went with what felt right. For her, that was to be Ethel—a strong woman who cared and stood up for others she noticed were suffering. That choice to be completely herself, without fear influencing every action, ultimately led to her embrace of being a Black woman. In this biography, I tell the story of Ethel's rites of passage from birth to the age of 23, when she left Duluth for other opportunities. I also share the backstory of her family and several events that shaped all of them through narrative, insightful journal entries and riveting poetry written by Lenny Prater. A look into Ethel's family is required to understand how fear and hesitation can change the course of how one sees their identity. It only makes sense to start with her parents, who nurtured their children's conflicted spirits.

1

An Immigration/Migration Story in the North Star State

In 1888, William Henry Ray scoured the Twin Cities for work. At the time, Minneapolis, Minnesota, was experiencing rapid growth and industrialization. The city's economy was heavily dependent on the lumber, flour, and rail industries. With the growth of these industries came a demand for labor, particularly unskilled workers who could perform manual labor at a low wage.

African American men were seen as a source of cheap labor, and many were recruited from the southern United States to work in northern states. This was part of the legacy of slavery, a large population of African Americans fleeing the South to avoid treacherous conditions and threats to their lives.

As part of the Great Migration, social changes shapes employment opportunities for African Americans. William Henry found a job as a porter at Hotel Ardmore, one of the best hotels in the Minneapolis area. From the outside, everything was perfect for him. He was part of a fast-developing African American community in the Twin Cities and was being paid well, until he found himself in a situation where he had to flee the dangers of racist men after falling deeply in love with Inga Nordquist, a Swedish immigrant.

William Henry knew of the horrors of the deep South. During his early life in North Carolina, he had witnessed lynchings of Black men for reasons no other than being Black, showing some dignity, or even looking at a white man or woman. Having lost their father and mother, William Henry's older sisters, Peggy and Rachel, believed it would be safer for their ten-year-old brother to move out of North

Carolina up North to a place like Ohio, which was known for having some safe spaces for Black migrants. The sisters felt if they did not do something, William Henry would most likely end up being lynched. He could already read and write, thanks to northern whites who had come down to North Carolina and started several schools to teach the newly freed. His sisters could feel the noose slipping around his neck just from the fact he was more articulate and smarter than most of the white men around them. William Henry begrudgingly agreed to leave his family, accompanying some of the people who previously had ensured safe passage on the former Underground Railroad. This trek took William Henry several years. First, he lived and went to school in Ohio. Later, he lived with the Claussens, his German adoptive family, in Davenport, Iowa, before finally arriving in Minnesota at the age of 20.

•••

Young William Henry Ray, circa 1880s

Tuesday, December 11th, 1888

I was a farm girl from Sweden who knew nothing at all about this country, or what prejudice was, or anything like that . . . I just knew some English.

-Inga

When Inga Nordquist was eighteen, she left Sweden and came to the United States to join her brother, Louis. Employers wanted cheap help from Europe, and many immigrant girls got jobs in big hotels as maids. Louis set Inga up with a job at Hotel Ardmore as a live-in laundress. Here, she met my great-grandfather. William Henry was the first man of color Inga had ever laid eyes on, and according to her, he bewitched her with his incredible good looks. She slowly became aware of the social attitudes against a couple like theirs. Her Swedish relatives didn't approve of their relationship, and Inga noticed the grimaces when they were together in public. She just wasn't aware of what that disdain could possibly amount to for her partner and herself.

Tuesday, January 10th, 1888 - Hotel Ardmore

I met a man who could be described as handsome without a doubt. The first Black man that I've ever made significant eye contact with, and he looked at me with such strong brown eyes. It was with such-what's the word-allure. I'll always remember the first time our hands touched. It spread a fire within me and I did nothing to stop him from fanning the flames. His name is William Henry Ray, but my brother Louis doesn't like him very much. I think it's because he's a negro, but now that I'm here in America, I think I should be able to like whoever I want. That man might just get me into trouble one of these days.

-Inga

Wednesday, December 18th, 1889

I knew it was dangerous, and if I had ever dared to do even a sliver of what I had done with Inga in the South, I'd been swinging from a tree two months ago. But I'm a man who gets what he sets his eyes on and she was so sweet on me. Inga started to feel a bit sick in the morning and I knew then that I had to marry the woman and get moving. There was a lot to be tolerated up here in the cities, but I had a feeling no one would be as accepting of this.

-William Henry

William Henry and Inga Ray, 1889

With the feeling of trouble tightening around his throat, William Henry married Inga in May 1890—but he knew he would still have to run. The idea of a Black man with a white woman even in Minneapolis had its repercussions. William Henry felt, from the hostility he received from his coworkers and other community folk, that it was a matter of time before a northern noose would be tied around his neck. So he ran again, like he had as a boy from North Carolina, but this time he ran even farther north to Duluth, Minnesota, with his wife in one hand and a rifle in the other.

Inga Nordquist and William Henry Ray were socially illegal lovers. Even Inga's Swedish relatives felt uneasy about their relationship, and their union was beyond taboo in an American society rampant with racism, yet still they chose each other. It is easy to believe they ended up together due to destiny: A white girl in her teens crosses the waters from the Land of the Midnight Sun and destiny directs that she marries a young Black man from the segregated South.

William Henry and Inga's first child, William "Will" Nordquist Ray, was born in Duluth in June 1890. Soon afterward, the new family moved another thirty miles up the shore of Lake Superior to Two Harbors, a small town with a population of around a thousand people. The town economy centered around shipping and mining, with many families depending on these industries for their livelihoods. Many children from working-class families worked in the mines or on the docks to help support their families. Here William Henry and Inga obtained jobs in a boardinghouse.

As the boardinghouse keeper in Two Harbors, William Henry was responsible for managing and maintaining the house, which was a type of lodging that provided temporary accommodations for travelers and workers. Some of the duties he shared with Inga were cleaning and maintenance, which included tasks such as sweeping, mopping, dusting, laundering linens and towels, and preparing and serving meals. William Henry was also responsible for collecting rent from guests, managing expenses, and keeping track of financial records. He was the point of contact for guests and was responsible for ensuring their needs were met and any issues or complaints addressed. Who would've thought someone would put a Negro in charge of such administrative responsibilities?

The family lived in Two Harbors from 1890 to 1898. Their daughter Ora Inga Ray was born in 1893 and their son Oscar Edwin Ray in 1895. Inga was always exhausted with the duties of the boardinghouse as well as the care of three children five years old and under. When William Henry learned that Inga was pregnant with their fourth child, Ethel, he decided it was time to move, plant some roots, and create some real stability for his family.

Sunday, February 6th, 1898

I purchased a house in Duluth and Inga is near the end of her fourth pregnancy. There are two approaches to Duluth-the front door, across St. Louis Bay when the hills rise abruptly from the water's edge up to the sky, one gradual ascent from Lake Superior and St. Louis Bay, or one can come by way of the "back entrance" through the farming country of Minnesota, Rush City, Moose Lake, Carlton, when you climb gradually to the top of the hill and descend Thompson Hill into the city proper. Thompson Hill is the kind of hill that car drivers bragged about in the winter before modern engineering removed some of the steepness: "I made Thompson Hill in high!" And the question invariably followed: "What were you driving?" That reply authenticated or dismissed the boast as to its worth. Some cars simply couldn't stand the long hill without attaining a speed that could not be maintained because of sharp corners and sudden curves. And the sheet of ice that was the usual winter dress, and fog off the lake, made descending Thompson Hill the last ride

```
for many daring drivers. It took great skill
and long familiarity in manipulation to
conquer its contour like bus drivers.
```
–William Henry

William Henry and Inga found ways to build a life and community in Duluth. Their last child, Ethel May Ray, was born here on April 13, 1899. They connected with other African American families in the area and also found support from sympathetic white allies working to promote racial equality and social justice. However, Minnesota was not immune to the racism and segregation prevalent throughout the United States during the late nineteenth century, and African Americans in Duluth faced many of the same challenges, such as finding or buying a home, as those in other parts of the country.

Before the Homeowners Association
(HOA)

Word on the street there are people lookin' for trouble
Tryna muck up the neighborhood prosiness
With their (mu)la(tt)o and poor excuse of
A matrimony void of holiness.

Tryna muck up the neighborhood prosiness,
So we greet them with the water from our hoses.
We all know it's a marriage void of holiness,
So why should we have to sit back with upturned noses?

Greet them with the water from our hoses
And maybe they'll be washed away.
Why should we have to sit back with upturned noses
While they taint Duluth like a couple of strays?

Maybe they'll be washed away
With water that will make their lungs bubble
Instead of tainting Duluth like a couple of strays.
Word on the street there's niggers lookin' for trouble.

Together, the family managed the best they could around their white counterparts. There was no shortage of cold stares and ruthless bullying for the kids. For Ora, this racism ended up being lethal.

In 1900, seven-year-old Ora became bedridden with pneumonia. Hospitals in Duluth were limited in terms of their resources and capacity and were not able to provide intensive care or specialized treatment for pneumonia, nor could William Henry's salary afford hospitalization, so Ora's treatment took place in their home. Inga provided supportive care for Ora and did her best to ensure her daughter was comfortable by providing fluids and nourishment and monitoring her symptoms for signs of deterioration.

As soon as she saw Ora's condition worsening, Inga had her husband summon the doctor. William Henry was home from work when the doctor arrived. The doctor was startled to see a Black man with a white wife and four interracial children. He was quick to write out a prescription for Ora's medication without examining her. He gave the parents instructions on how often and how much medicine to administer before leaving abruptly. Ora died a few days later.

Though Ethel was only a small child herself when Ora passed, years later she still felt the effects of her sister's untimely death.

Wednesday, October 1st, 1913

Today is a sad day because Ora died on this day. It's been 13 years since my big sister's death and I really don't remember her as I was only 18 months old when she died. Mom said that Ora liked to tell me stories while in bed too sick to move. It seemed she liked to have me around and would ask for me a lot. I think my sister loved me.

They think she died because the medicine the doctor gave was too strong. Father wanted Ora to take it exactly how the doctor said even though she cried and said it burned. Mom said Ora didn't like when dad check-in on her because he forced her to take the medicine.

Father said he never should have trusted the doctor and he will never again trust any doctor blindly.

My parent's told me to their surprise, when the doctor came back, he scolded them and said the medicine was too strong for a sick child and should have been diluted. This further made my father lose faith in doctors and we rarely had one in the house. Mother tells us Ora seemed glad to die when she realized she could not get better.

According to my mom, one of her friends said that Ora may have been better off dead, as her life would have been a hard one in this world, being a mulatto and all. From what I was told Ora was passive like Mom. Naturally, both mom and dad took the death hard.

-Ethel

    Ethel's father managed to capture significant moments in the family's lives through photographs. When they laid Ora to rest, he encapsulated the grief his wife and children felt in a photograph. He placed it above the fireplace, and every day, it greeted them with the quote "Lest we forget." This phrase is taken from Rudyard Kipling's 1897 poem "Recessional." This photograph and phrase served as a constant reminder of the pain they experienced saying goodbye to Ora.

*Will, Inga, and Oscar after the funeral of Ora
(Photo by William Henry, 1900)*

Who Poisoned Me?

With his big black coils, skin like the soot in
our wood oven, he convinced the doctor
Who was stark white in his soul and skin that
There was no antidote for a niglet.

Why did Daddy poison me with a coffee
Tinted lacquer in the womb? My mother's
drop of cream wasn't enough to save me.
My drink was doomed from the beginning, Ma.

A dirty little nigger like me was
Sure to taint gloveless hands. He told my sweet
Mother that I was meant to die and went
On until my blood stained her timid hands.

It isn't because Dad stayed home. It was
obvious that my blood was unholy
In the eyes of their white god, we bend our
Knees for at church, glass stained and almighty.

For the remaining Ray children, living up north was certainly different from where William Henry had grown up in North Carolina. The South may have been a dangerous place to be Black, but at least he had been surrounded by a community of other Black folks. Ethel and her brothers, Will and Oscar, spent a great deal of time with each other, as they found it difficult to integrate with others whose families often disapproved of them and did not allow them in their homes, and many times would not allow them to play or interact with their children.

William Henry met and became friends with John Beargrease, a legendary figure in the history of Minnesota's North Shore. Born in 1858 fifty miles north of Duluth in Beaver Bay, Mr. Beargrease grew up in a family of Ojibwe and was raised in the traditional ways of his people. His father, Chief Moquabimetem, who also went by the name "Beargrease," had been a renowned dog musher hired by the American Fur Company to deliver mail and supplies to remote outposts. Mr. Beargrease gained a reputation as a skilled and reliable mail carrier too. He was also known for his kindness and willingness to help others. He often carried supplies and messages for people along his route, and he would stop and check on people who were sick or in need. Over time, Mr. Beargrease's reputation grew, and he became a beloved figure in the communities along his route. People began to refer to him as the Great Northern Mail Carrier, and he became a symbol of resilience and determination in the face of harsh North Shore winters.

William Henry's family and Mr. Beargrease's family shared a warm relationship. Ethel and her brothers were always excited to watch him use a rowboat and a dogsled to deliver the mail. Beargrease would sometimes bring his oldest daughters, Charlotte and MaryAnn, along to assist him. Other times, his mother, Newagagamsbag (or Otoe), would accompany him. Mr. Beargrease and his daughters would often come into their home to eat, but his mother insisted on staying outside no matter how cold. It was obvious she was hesitant about interacting with this Black man, his white wife, and their children. William Henry and Inga were always kind and hospitable and wondered why Mr. Beargrease's mother would not enter their home.

They would ask, "Why don't you bring your mother in sometime? I thought you were going to bring her in?" It turns out she just refused.

William Henry loved to share stories with his kids about his adventures with John Beargrease and the other Native Americans in Two Harbors. When hunting together, Mr. Beargrease shared stories about his life and experiences with William Henry. He spoke of his love for the land and his respect for the animals he hunted. William Henry developed a deep respect for his friend's way of life and his peoples' connection to the land. This connection led him to recall the life he had lived in North Carolina and Iowa before coming to Duluth, and he tried to remember if his people also had a similar relationship with the land before they were enslaved and forced to work it for free.

Ethel and her brothers did not have many friends in Duluth, but they were no strangers to the Native children. With them, they could be their full selves. They played together and did not see any differences between themselves and the Native children. They were all just kids being "wild and free."

This kinship was not true anywhere else. At school and out in their immediate neighborhood, the Ray children began to form ideas of what it meant to be of mixed heritage, of what having a Black father and white mother meant in the context of their world. These ideas planted seeds of doubt in their minds of whether these differences made others better than them. After all, their mother was not just white; her people were Nordic, of Northern European descent. Most white people, including Inga, viewed individuals from the Scandinavian countries (Sweden, Norway, Denmark, and Finland) as having superior intelligence, physical strength, and moral character compared to people from other regions of the world. After Inga mentioned this to her proud Black Southern husband, William Henry insisted that, under his watchful eye, "Black superiority" would be the doctrine of their household. Growing up in the South and fleeing to the North, he was fully aware that white men did not live up to this imaginary image they tried so hard to make everyone believe. If there was anything William Henry felt sure he could control, it was his family. This control would occasionally translate into what felt like a stifling strictness waged against Ethel's brothers, Will and Oscar.

Ethel witnessed Oscar take blows from their dad in the name of discipline. Will most likely had similar experiences, but because he was nine years older than her, she never witnessed those exchanges. Their mother tried her best to intervene because she was sure her husband would kill Oscar in his wrath. William Henry was usually sorry—to a degree—afterward. Ethel found herself harboring bad feelings toward her father as he started to feel like just another one of the bad people in her life who caused them harm for no clear reason.

Thursday, February 26th, 1914

```
I can remember my mother tiptoeing quietly
to my bed and warning me not to go to sleep
because she was afraid. I wasn't totally
without fear and recall lying in bed,
holding my breath, not moving, listening as
those footsteps came up the stairs, listening,
waiting, my heart pounding away inside,
waiting to hear the first word when the door
was opened to learn whether it would be a
night of Hell or a night of rest-Mother has
never known (until recently) how near I was
to her, especially at those times-to her I
seemed to be hard, never outwardly
portraying my emotions.
```

-Ethel

Inga became a protector for the kids, and her whiteness made it all the more effective. Imagine a white woman in her front yard with her child covered in bruises by her Black husband. What was already frowned upon would have escalated into an angry mob at their front door. It was never mentioned that William Henry hit Inga in the process of her trying to look out for her children, but the chances of domestic abuse would've been higher if he'd been married to a Black woman.

William Henry wasn't hard on Ethel in the same way he was on Oscar. She was frequently ill as a child, and this frailty might have suggested the possibility of a shortened life. In her father's scheme of things, he knew he would be devastated if he was to lose another child.

The tradition of Black families putting fear into their children has direct ties to slavery. Black parents lived in fear of any perceived slight toward white people, which could result in the death of their children. Black people have experienced generations of mental and physical trauma that has taught them that inflicting pain on someone is the key to making them "act right." To make someone fear disobeying rules or fear not being as topnotch as possible—that is the best way to get through to someone because it paralyzes them. Violence is a simple way to keep people in line. When multiple generations are taught that violence works, it can be incredibly hard to escape. Unfortunately, William Henry continued that cycle.

At the turn of the twentieth century, racial segregation and discrimination were rampant in many parts of American society, including housing, education, and employment. The concept of racial purity was also ingrained in the minds of many, and mixed-race individuals were often stigmatized and marginalized. These families faced significant social and economic challenges, including discrimination and harassment from white communities but also nuanced ill treatment from those in the Black community.

The Ray family house kept their children hidden from the outside world. It was as if they were in a perpetual state of quarantine. Neighbors across the street, behind them, and to both sides of them were racist and made it clear they despised the family and did not want them to inhale the air high on the hill. All outings were planned, nothing impromptu. The kids either accompanied their parents to an activity or attended school or church or spent time with friends who had been screened by their parents.

William Henry was aware of the limits the racist environment posed on his family and other Black families. Even before the death of his baby girl Ora, he knew the treatment they received was the bare minimum of tolerance. He knew if anything happened, the Black people in his town would not be safe, nor have any way to protect themselves and their families.

William Henry began his activism and attempted to establish a NAACP chapter in Duluth in the early 1900's, but many Black residents were opposed. They were afraid it would cause conflict that did not exist, even though a Ku Klux Klan chapter was headquartered in downtown Duluth just blocks from the police station. Little did they know there was trouble on the horizon and William Henry had every reason to be concerned in the northern town of Duluth.

2

The Formative Years and Young Adulthood

All three of the remaining Ray children had differing educational experiences. Will, the oldest, was eight years old when his family left Two Harbors and he struggled to ever feel grounded in Duluth. When living in Two Harbors, he had not attended school. Will and his siblings spent most of his time playing with the neighboring Native American children. In Duluth, Will's parents enrolled him in a segregated school, Franklin Elementary, where his fair complexion allowed him to pass as white. He was the only person of mixed race pictured in his class photograph. All the other children and teachers were white. Despite not attending school during his early years, Will kept up with his classmates and later attended Duluth's Central High School in 1905. Central High was an integrated school; at the time Will attended, he then identified as a Black student. He faced challenges and discrimination that limited his opportunities for academic and personal success. Exclusion from extracurricular activities and social events, as well as verbal and physical harassment from white peers, created a hostile learning environment, yet Will was able to complete and graduate from Central High.

Oscar struggled in school, not only because of racial discrimination but also internally. He had a hard time learning and fell behind in multiple grades. He struggled with his inability to grow as tall or as athletic as his brother, Will. Ethel surpassed him both physically, growing taller than him, and educationally at the age of sixteen. Oscar grew too embarrassed to continue high school and chose to drop out in his freshman year at the age of twenty-one after discovering he would have to repeat ninth grade yet another year. It is believed Oscar suffered from physical and cognitive disabilities that were not diagnosable at the time. His pride took an irrecoverable beatdown.

There was very little in Duluth for young people. There was one historical Black church at the time, St. Mark's African Methodist Episcopal (AME). Ethel went there occasionally, but her father wanted his children to become regular in their religious habits so he preferred they go to the integrated Episcopal church. There, he said, they would learn regularity and discipline.

Ethel had her share of hostile experiences at school. She was the only student of color at Franklin when she entered, as her brothers had already finished elementary school. She was not able to pass as white like Will or Oscar, since her skin was of a darker complexion and she had kinky hair. Even at the young age of five, she was exposed to unfair and racist attitudes. Her desk was placed in the very back of the classroom in the corner. These discriminatory experiences were consistent throughout her early years. This included being cast in a play in which she was the only person of color. Although she was one of the younger and smaller students, she was chosen for the role of wicked stepmother.

Thursday, February 21st, 1918

When I was seven years old, I was in the play "One Eye, Two Eye & Three Eye." In this Grimms fairy tale, the oldest daughter was named One Eye since she had one eye in the middle of her forehead; the second was Two Eye, because she looked like other people, and Three-Eye earned her name as she had a third eye in the middle of her forehead. As the stepmother, I disliked Two Eyes because she was not special like One and Three eyes. So the story tells of how, as the Stepmother, I mistreated Two Eyes by pushing her about and tossing her worn clothes to wear.

> For my costume, I wore spectacles, an apron, and a long shirt, with my hair done as an old woman twisted at the back of the head in a plain coil. The other girls got to dress up really nicely with white dresses and beautiful bows in their hair. I was the only person of color in the play, so it was ironic that I was chosen to be the "wicked stepmother" who mistreated her stepchild because she was not unique like her sisters when in fact, I tried to live my life contrary to my portrayal in the play.
>
> —Ethel

As Ethel recalled the events of her early life, she concluded that the complexities and difficulties presented as a member of an interracial family in a small Minnesotan town were made easier to bear through her connection with the church. Dr. Albert Ryan, the minister of the integrated St. Paul Episcopal Church, was very tolerant of young people, including Ethel. She found freedom in the church, and the regimentation of church routine did not present any hardship after the strict discipline she was used to at home. Seven or eight girls constituted the core of the young people in the Sunday School, and they remained intact throughout her elementary and high school years, providing Ethel with a cohort of peers. They became a mainstay of helpers when necessary. These experiences helped Ethel develop leadership qualities useful later in her life.

Ethel's father approved the discipline of the established Episcopal church, although he did not attend. William Henry often spoke, deploringly, of the lack of continuity in Duluth's one Black Methodist church, St. Mark's AME, where sometimes there was Sunday School and sometimes not, because of a lack of teachers. It was understood in the Ray household that Sundays included attendance at Sunday School unless illness prevented, and then Ethel stayed home. She attended St. Mark's when she wished but only after the regular Sunday School at St. Paul Episcopal. During her high school days, Ethel was elected president of the Philathea Class, the young people's group in the Episcopal church.

Ethel and her brothers were the only African Americans at St. Paul Episcopal for a long time. They were eventually joined by another boy and his sister for a short period. Dr. Ryan's influence must have generated a friendly environment compared to other white churches.

World War I started in 1914, the United States voted to enter the war in 1917. Both Will and Oscar enlisted in World War I in 1918. They both ended up in France after the end of the war in 1919. After seeing her brothers leave not just the state, but the country, Ethel's desire to leave Duluth grew.

Prior to graduation, Ethel watched a close white friend of hers named Adaline quit high school after she acquired a full-time job at a department store. Ethel, on the other hand, was advised to stay in school by her family and friends. She couldn't quit school to work even if she wanted to, as there were little to no job opportunities in Duluth for Negroes. On June 13, 1917, just two months after the start of America's involvement in World War I, Ethel graduated from Central High School in the assembly hall. She held onto the graduation program from which her name was inauspiciously absent. However, her senior class picture appeared in the yearbook with her accomplishments listed alongside. Her many accomplishments included learning stenography (a note taking technique) and having near perfect scores on the civil service examination.

Friday, September 28th, 1917

At home we didn't really discuss me going to college. During my job search, it became blatant the discrimination I would face in the workforce. When I started hunting for work, I saw how easy it was for the white girls from school to get placed in department stores and offices. Every opportunity seemed to magically disappear when I tried to apply. Luckily, a neighbor helped me get temporary jobs like typing and

> copying election lists. I located a friend in one of the Liberty Loan Drive offices who agreed to hire me. This was a short-term assignment, but at least I made some contacts I could use for future references.
>
> —Ethel

In October 1918, the year after Ethel graduated from high school, disastrous forest fires took the lives of more than five hundred people in northern Minnesota; injured about two thousand people; caused more than thirty million dollars in property damage; and devastated several entire communities as well as a million acres of forestland. Over eleven thousand families became homeless refugees. More than four thousand homes, and over six thousand other buildings, were destroyed. Workers were needed at the emergency relief headquarters in Duluth. The governor appointed a Minnesota Forest Fire Relief Commission to work in cooperation with the American Red Cross. Colonel Hubert V. Eva, the state director, was in charge.

Calls went out from Moose Lake for volunteers, and Ethel applied. Luckily, she had worked under Colonel Eva during the Liberty Loan Drive. He hired her immediately upon her arrival at headquarters as an investigator to interview refugees and as a stenographer in Moose Lake, forty miles southwest of Duluth. Ethel worked in this capacity from October 1918 to March 1919. Her duties, along with many other volunteers, included checking emergency relief centers and hospitals for lists of survivors and morgues for lists of the dead, with whatever descriptions were available. Information was sparse, such as a "few inches of a braid of blond hair," "a small piece of a gingham dress," "part of a shoe." Food, clothing, and shelter were priorities. In addition to her work as an investigator and stenographer, Ethel worked with Charles F. Mahnke, the Editor of the Moose Lake Star Gazette.

The same year as the forest fires, an influenza epidemic closed the schools. Since schools were closed, teachers were drafted into service to locate and interview refugees. They reported each morning for their daily assignments. Ethel ended up running into her former third grade teacher, who had discriminated against her when she was younger. This teacher was now assigned under Ethel, who supervised her and gave her daily appointments. Ethel doubted this woman had any recollection of who she was as she did not appear to recognize her. Nonetheless, the irony was not lost on Ethel.

After the assignment ended, Ethel went back home to Duluth looking for work. A couple of months later, Charles F. Mahnke, who was also the local director of the forest fire relief commission, had a position open in Moose Lake. A worker from Chicago had become ill en route to Moose Lake, so Ethel volunteered to go back down to serve temporarily. She had previously worked for Mr. Mahnke, as his secretary assisting with his work as the editor of the Moose Lake Star-Gazette weekly newspaper. He was also chairman of the school board, chairman of a building committee for the Methodist church, and a representative of the Federal Loan Bank.

Moose Lake was a community that had been seriously hit by the tragedy and held the highest mortality rate in the state. The forest fires had leveled the town, like the images that had come out of World War I's devastated cities in Europe. Temporary barracks were built for housing and for office quarters. The town was under the military jurisdiction of the Minnesota Home Guard.

After her temporary assignment ended, Mr. Mahnke asked Ethel to return for a permanent assignment in Moose Lake. Ethel's parents reluctantly agreed since the opportunity would provide her with valuable work experience; however, William Henry thought the people of Moose Lake were getting exactly what they deserved for being the most racist stop on the railroad for Black men who worked the route from Duluth to Minneapolis. His stance was by no means an unusual occurrence. Moose Lake was known by many to be a racist town, but Ethel, left with limited options, had to work wherever opportunity arose.

Ethel lived in Moose Lake for about three years, from 1919 to 1922. The state was divided into fire relief districts, and weekly meetings were held at headquarters in Duluth to bring together all directors in charge of area relief. Although social workers had been brought in from all over the country, the flu epidemic kept the working force seriously understaffed, so Ethel was able to visit home only on rare occasions.

The workers were kept busy by the lines of people coming into the office for food, clothing, and lumber to build temporary homes. Below-zero temperatures made it necessary to work in topcoats until wood fires could be started each morning in the offices. Ink wells were frozen, and typewriter keys refused to respond to touch until midday.

While Ethel lived in Moose Lake, she attended the local Methodist church since the Episcopal church held services only once a month. She became active in Sunday School and played the organ. She was eventually elected president of the Epworth League, the Methodist young people's organization. The young people at the church in Moose Lake were active in giving programs for other organizations and in adjoining towns. Ethel also became president of another group called the Loyal Chums.

Despite all of her experiences and skills, like most Black students, Ethel did not have a chance at earning a scholarship or gaining entrance into college without a recommendation of someone highly prestigious. The Moose Lake Episcopalian Sunday Schools superintendent, Mrs. Elva Jackman, wrote to New York to secure permission for Ethel's selection for admission. Mrs. Jackman became interested in Ethel's potential and contacted the state Sunday School Association in an attempt to get a scholarship for her to attend college.

The superintendent of Sunday Schools at the Episcopalian church in Duluth came and spoke to Ethel after hearing about Mrs. Jackman's inquiry. He interviewed Ethel and stated that if she desired to go to college, arrangements could be made at the Episcopal Institute in New York City or the religiously affiliated branch of Boston University. When she inquired if they assisted graduates with employment, he replied that she would probably be assigned to work with the Indians in northern Minnesota or the Negroes in Asheville, North Carolina. His response felt discriminatory due to the fact that hundreds of employment opportunities around the country were available, but not to her because she was Black. This discouraged her, and she "filed" the matter. Ethel's parents didn't approve of either the Boston or the New York offer, as they didn't want her too far from home.

Ethel didn't notice the discrimination so much until the fire aftermath settled down and people started having their social events again. There was a women's life insurance society called the Degree of Honor Club, and some members pressured her to join. She wasn't interested, but it was something to do. Ethel was quite lonely. The local barber, a man from Kentucky, told the women his wife couldn't belong as long as a Negro was in the club, but the ladies who proposed her name insisted on Ethel's acceptance.

And then there were the people who "knew" Ethel could sing and fry chicken because "all Negroes do and can!" One evening she was invited to go with a group of young people to "coon" melons, which meant going out to the country and helping yourself to melons in farmers' fields. Ethel didn't go.

A dentist in an adjoining office used to come to the relief center and tell stories about Negroes. He insisted Negroes did not have white teeth—it was merely their Blackness that caused their teeth to look white. Actually, he stated, "Negroes' teeth are almost always yellow." He had been on stage once, impersonating the black minstrel, and liked giving demonstrations.

Ethel felt fortunate that Mr. Mahnke exhibited no prejudice toward her or any other racial group. He was respectful of the town's only Jewish family, who ran the clothing store, and of the many Finnish immigrant farmers living outside town who knew little English. They all seemed to trust him and came to him in many emergencies. Mr. Mahnke expressed satisfaction with Ethel's work, which made the situation in Moose Lake bearable. However, life outside of work was unbearably lonely.

The Pilgrimage (December 1919 to March 1920)

Negro college students would come to Duluth during the summer months to work on the docks by the ships. Ethel remembered some arrived on ships named the Juanita and the Kionesta. Duluth sits on a hill about a mile high and fourteen miles long, at the southwest point of Lake Superior. It was a pretty sight to see the boats arrive and leave. There was a great deal of difference between Duluth, Minnesota, and Superior, Wisconsin. They were called the Twin Ports.

Superior was just across the St. Louis Bay bridge. Superior was populated mostly by Germans, who generally had a better feeling toward Black people than the Scandinavian population of Duluth. There weren't too many Blacks in Superior, but there weren't too many Blacks anywhere the Rays grew up. Young people went away because there was nothing much for them to do.

There were few gatherings. The Rays used to go to a place called the Point. It was a strip of land across the Aerial Bridge on Lake Superior. Many Duluth residents liked to go across the bridge and have picnics; however, growing up in the Ray household, Ethel and her brothers could not use the term "picnic." William Henry explained to his children it was code for "picking a nigga to lynch," although this meaning probably developed in the Black community as the "sport" of lynching became more prominent. But aside from the Sunday school gatherings, or a few families getting together, there wasn't much for young people. It was a bit better when teenagers would have their little dances and house parties. In the summertime, students from Howard, Fisk, and other schools south of them would spend the day in Duluth and their nights in Superior. There would be matinee dances where the mothers would chaperone, which was a very nice thing for Ethel and her friends.

William Henry most likely knew Ethel was his only child who didn't care to pass as white, regardless of whether she could or not. To avoid any chance of her planting that self-destructive seed in her head, William Henry took his daughter on an extended trip across the country and down South. It was a perfectly timed pick-me-up for his daughter, who struggled to get on with the subtle discrimination her white counterparts offered every day. Ethel needed to know where her father came from and appreciate the good fight Black folk like himself had made for their children. So he made it an educational trip while also intending for her to meet distant relatives. They traveled to Chicago, Illinois; Detroit, Michigan; Toledo, Ohio; Cincinnati, Ohio; Rochester, New York; Boston, Massachusetts; New Haven, Connecticut; Buffalo, New York; New York City; Philadelphia, Pennsylvania; Baltimore, Maryland; Richmond, Virginia; Charlotte, Raleigh, and Durham, North Carolina; and Atlanta, Georgia. This was a life-changing experience for Ethel.

Her mother did not want Ethel to go. Inga knew it wasn't safe for a Black girl in Duluth but feared what could happen to her daughter in the South. She had heard stories of why her husband fled the South and the terrible discrimination he faced. But William Henry said they were going, and the two of them went.

Seed to Root

Was it the presentation of roots?
A sign that it was reckless to abandon
the depth that fed them

Maybe it was the promise that they could
  grow their own
With the opportunity to have stories to seed
And shared names across miles acted as
  fertilizer

It was the toil
The surprise at first bud
The sharpness of thorns

It was love
It was curiosity
It was Ethel.

It was Ethel.
A sapling ready for rings.
It had to be Ethel,
a root bearer unafraid to branch.

Chicago

Tuesday, December 16th, 1919

Our train was late, so it was about a quarter after the noon hour when we pulled into the Soo Station of the Windy City. This was my first real glimpse of a real city with real tall buildings and crowded streets. So this was the city I had heard and read so much about. All this hurry and noise went with it evidently.

-Ethel

Friday, December 19th, 1919

When arriving in Chicago my dad and I were greeted by no one. After visiting a few friends, we went over to the Illinois Central Station and I marveled at the look of it. At first glimpse, it looked as though it would be up to us to fill in part of old Lake Superior if they wanted to move something like it up to Duluth. Next on the program was the Art Gallery. I wished I lived right around the corner from it and could run over every now and then. I love painting and I knew going there could give me lots of valuable techniques for painting. My dad and I then took a tour of the Y.M.C.A. on 38th and Wabasha courtesy of Mr. Frayser T. Lane, the Secretary. I didn't know anything of the sort could exist for Black folk. I adored the shiny basketball floor and imagined sliding right across it, but supposed I would have mortified my dad and shocked Mr. Lane. I wondered if I would have to act dignified during our whole trip but kept my impulses to myself most times.

-Ethel

Friday, December 26th, 1919

My dad gave me a huge stack of The Chicago Defender, the Negro newspaper. He said when he was a porter that he would always get stacks of the Negro newspapers from the major cities because that was how the community around the country received their information about what's really going on. He said we will sell them along our trip and give some out too. He highly encouraged me to read them too.

-Ethel

Boston

Saturday, January 3rd, 1920

We arrived in Boston, at 9:15 a.m. This looks like a real city, believe me. We met Mr. Booker, a mason, who directed us to some of his friends. We were taken by taxi to Helen R. Lindsey at 588 Columbus Avenue. They live in quite a big apartment house. This was the first time I have ever stayed in one like this. No outsiders, only my own people. We found Mrs. Lindsey and her daughter very friendly and made us very much at home. The pillows sure felt good not having been in a real bed since before we left home.

-Ethel

Monday, January 12th, 1920

I learned not to ever travel without a well-sharpened pencil and a notebook. I could hardly recall the street names. My father and I visited the Shaw monument on the Commons and also the statue erected to Crispus Attucks and his companions who fell in the Boston Massacre. We also visited the place further downtown that was marked with a star in the middle of the street. It marked the exact spot where he fell. I thought it showed the democratic spirit of the Bostonians, and thought well of them. Saturday morning Helen went with us to Faneuil Hall market. It was the first time I had ever seen such an enormous market. It was about two blocks long inside with fresh meats of every description and name lined up on each side of the aisle. There were carts and wagons with vendors selling everything from peanuts to suits of clothes outdoors. The narrow streets made them seem more crowded than they really were. It was a long line of one-way streets down into town, so it was called Market Street.

-Ethel

Saturday, January 17th, 1920

One morning, my dad and I visited Ebenezer Baptist Church a few blocks away. Mr. Isaiah Hawking joined us. Reverend Ward was the pastor and a very able one at that. You wouldn't find one eyelid start to fall during his sermons. He seemed very well-versed along historical lines. After church, we walked home, visiting the Public Library. I thought of it with the same marvel as everything else I had seen so far. We passed the Trinity Cathedral, Parker House, stopped at the Art Museum, and ended our exploration at Buck Bay Station before heading home.

-Ethel

New York

Saturday, January 24th, 1920

My dad and I took the Interurban over to Niagara Falls. We took pictures and could only hope that they turned out good. I couldn't believe how scenic it had been. We met a man, Mr. Marsh, out here who was also taking pictures. He was kind enough to snap some photographs of us. His home is in Hot Springs, Arkansas, and was employed at the Shredded Wheat Factory. My dad and I went through the factory and found everything extremely sanitary, interesting, and appetizing. My dad said that he wouldn't mind eating shredded wheat at all now after seeing how it was made. We were shown the entire process, from the wheat seed until the time it was in the box to the way they bought it in the store. Afterward, we returned to Buffalo and left for New York City. From Grand Central Station, we left for Philly as our next destination. While in New York, my father grabbed a stack of The Amsterdam News, another Negro newspaper, for me to hold and take to our next stop.

-Ethel

Charlotte

Sunday, February 1st, 1920

When arriving in North Carolina, we stopped at Charlotte, for a short time to see the beautiful buildings in the capital city. Of course, we pick up the Charlotte Post to see what's been going on with Negros around the state. We went to Raleigh and stopped in to get a look at the land my father inherited. We didn't do much there as it was empty, so we traveled further to Durham to meet family. Bessie, a distant cousin, met up with us, and we walked about a mile to our house together. I was happy to see Bessie after corresponding with her for over ten years. The next day we went to town and visited the National Training School where Viola, another relative, attended.

-Ethel

Friday, February 13th, 1920

The whole week we were kept busy meeting and visiting cousins. There were almost too many to count, and I was sure I could have counted some of them twice. I also got the opportunity to meet lots of my dad's old playmates and schoolmates. I was able to learn about a new side to my father, and it seemed like my dad did nothing but go to school and play in order to make all these people and stories fit in. I experienced a lot of firsts on the trip: staying in one and two-room cabins, bandana handkerchiefs, banjo, reels, mandolins, eating persimmons, and a thousand and one other things. I had a hard time keeping up with conversations. Our accents clashed, and sometimes it seemed as if we spoke different languages. We adapted however and I got closer to my family than I had ever imagined I would.

-Ethel

Friday, February 20th, 1919

The talk around town is that a Black man was hung earlier in February. I'm horrified. The authorities caught a young man accused of a crime and while in jail, a mob broke in, shot him to death, and then hung him. That makes no sense! To shoot a man, then hang him. No jury. No judge. No trial. They hated him so much they had to kill him twice. The body stayed up for days where thousands of white folks came and gawked at it. Of course, the police investigated and they could not determine who hung him. This is the pattern all around the country.

My dad said this is why he fled North Carolina. He said white folks often made-up unbelievable stories about Negroes. Many times, these stories led to their death. He said they would punish Negroes for being successful, for the sake of terrorism, and for simply being Black.

-Ethel

Monday, March 15th, 1919

There was always a number of people continually asking about the North. My father would explain and emphasize the advantages, especially for young people-so they could become better educated, etc. Many times, he would say, "You have the opportunity for schooling, you can get work, and while the white people don't exactly love you, the important thing is the law will protect you..."

-Ethel

Sunday, March 21st, 1920

After this amazing trip, I was forever changed. I must say, I now for the first time in my life understand my father. I learned so much from the places we went to, the people, the family, the community, the cities. The Negro was different in each place, but still a heaviness followed us all across the country. The world for Negros was a lot bigger than I had ever imagined living in our little home in Duluth. It was bigger than the Southern prejudices that sat in your throat like molasses every time a white person crossed your path. Hearing about that young man who was lynched when we were in North Carolina stayed with me. My only comfort was as my father said, "those kinda things don't happen up north and certainly not in Duluth."

-Ethel

3

Lynching Is as American as Apple Pie

Although lynching had been America's practice in maintaining fear and control since the country's founding in 1776, when the enslavement of African people was legal, the owners of African people did not see fit to lose their investments by destroying their "property." Black bodies were valuable commodities after they reached American soil. It wasn't until after the Civil War ended in 1865 and the physical freedom of enslaved Africans that a new level of terror was visited upon the barely freed. A Black body was no longer something to be commodified, so the torture a white man inflicted didn't have to stop at the brink of death. A white man could kill a Negro and there wasn't any good reason to stop him. After Reconstruction ended in 1877, Union troops were pulled out of the South, which allowed for the full reign of the Ku Klux Klan, and the frequency of the lynchings of Black men increased exponentially.

Ida B. Wells was a Black woman pioneer who documented lynchings across the country and gave the speech "Lynching, Our National Crime" in 1909. Her speech described 959 lynchings that occurred in the United States from 1899 to 1908. Of these, 102 were white, while Black people numbered 857. That correlated to about two Black men lynched every week during this nine-year period. In the summer of 1919, when Ethel was working in Moose Lake to help racist white communities recover from fires, it got so bad, so many Black people's deaths at the hands of whites, that it was referred to as the "Red Summer." This period of white supremist terrorism occurred in more than three dozen cities across the country. From 1882 to

1968, 4,743 lynchings occurred in the United States, according to records maintained by the NAACP. Of these, 72 percent lynched were Black. The myth of "race" and white supremacy created the ultimate taboo of a Black man violating the sacredness and pristineness of white women. The perpetuated narrative meant if a Black man even looked at a white woman, that would warrant immediate death.

Minnesota—and in particular Duluth, a populist northern city—was not exempt from the ethos of the lynching culture that permeated the rest of the country. Though Duluth's lynching story did not start in 1920, it was at its most potent then.

Billie Holiday sang of Southern trees bearing strange fruit, while Bob Dylan sang of postcards from the North displaying hangings of Black men in his song "Desolation Row." Murder by mob hanging was not a Southern phenomenon after all. On June 15, 1920, Duluth residents dragged, beat, and brutally hung three young Black men. Their bodies were not strung up from a poplar tree, or any other tree; nor were they hung in pastoral fields. The bodies of these nineteen- and twenty-year-old men, just out of boyhood, hung from a wooden telegraph post against the backdrop of a cityscape that included the large Shrine Temple. This happened here, in Minnesota, in a state as far North as one could get before crossing the border into Canada. Photos were taken at what was called "the necktie party," which signified how one stop during his journey could change, or rather end, the life of a Black circus worker, or any Black man for that matter.

The Circus is Coming to Town

Each year, Duluth hosted John Robinson's Circus, a Midwest family circus that lasted seventy-five years until 1917. It was bought by the American Circus Corporation, which was a conglomerate of other small regional circuses. In 1920, John Robinson's Circus, under new ownership and management, came to Duluth, Minnesota. This circus had all the typical elements: tents, trapeze artists, lions, tigers, elephants, clowns, and cotton candy. Back then, circuses moved almost every day and visited five to seven towns a week, with two performances a day. From the opening in spring until the close in late fall, there are not many days off for the circus workers.

It was strenuous to set up and tear down the tents and equipment. This work was left up to what was called "roustabouts." Often the circus traveled with twenty to fifty Black men who were primarily responsible for the hard labor and the worst jobs at the circus. Black roustabouts were segregated within those jobs and the trains. They were paid less than the white roustabouts and treated with some of the harshest forms of discrimination and racism. The show's destinations, in small towns throughout America, left them discriminated against and endangered. Although the public perception of circus employment often produces thoughts of fun and adventure, Black circus folk endured harsh treatment, low pay, and vile racism.

Segregation was easily accomplished in the circus, where the Black and white workers were always on the go and traveled in separate train cars. Black men were hired only as manual laborers, which included cleaning, cooking, and handling animals as dedicated stable boys. Much later, they were able to be musicians, but they were still paid as little as possible. Black circus workers were not seen as valuable workers. There was a circus train accident in 1892 where fourteen horses were killed but most of the Black roustabouts who shared a cart with them survived. The article covering the wreck led with the headline "Horses Better Than Negroes" because the manager was more upset over the loss of his horses than, in his words, some "darkies." The idea of a Black person's subhumanity thrived in the space of the circus world, and the expendability of some circus "niggers" was far from a secret to the white community.

DULUTH ONE DAY MONDAY, JUNE 14
AMERICA'S FIRST AND FOREMOST CIRCUS.
NOW THE FINEST IN THE WORLD.

JOHN ROBINSON'S CIRCUS

43 DENS WILD BEASTS 43
Herds of
PERFORMING ELEPHANTS
DROVES OF CAMELS
$1,000,000.00 BIG FREE STREET
PARADE DAILY AT 11 A.M.

SEE THE BIGGEST
BABY "CONGO"
THE HIPPOPOTAMUS
DOORS OPEN AT 1-7 P.M
PERFORMANCE STARTS 2-8 P.M

Admission and Reserved Seats on Sale Circus Day at Boyce's Drug Store. 331 West Superior Street. No extra charge.

African Dodgers

The African Dodger was a popular game in the circus industry. The game allowed players three chances to hit a Negro with a ball and win a prize. If permitted, the Negro would always be a real Black man, forced to stick his face through a hole and bait the pain. The game's popularity was equal to other exciting attractions and appeared in carnival advertisements alongside animals, illusionists, penny arcades, merry-go-rounds, and magic shows. "Dodgers" were what they were called, though one can assume they were never meant to dodge. The really unlucky ones made headlines for fractured noses or lost eyes. The articles were not meant to strike pity, instead providing even more entertainment for those who missed the moment in person. The five cents paid to hit them was not near enough to pay for a broken nose, but it wasn't like the men were given a share of the profits anyway.

In Duluth, it is not known what role Elias Clayton, Elmer Jackson, or Isaac McGhie served in the circus. But, based on what transpired the evening of June 15, 1920, their lives—like those Black men who were compared unfavorably to the horses lost—were not valued by the mob who snatched them from jail to deliver their own judgment and conviction, which was to beat, murder, and hang them from a telegraph post.

The Accusation

What led to the lynchings started well before the accusation of the three Black men who worked in the circus that stopped in Duluth. Irene Tusken was a white girl with an appetite for a thrill, who was dating a white boy, James Sullivan, despite her parents' disapproval. Michael Fedo, in his book The Lynchings in Duluth, describes James as a cocky boy who had little respect for the wishes of Irene's parents so the two of them snuck off to a ravine in Wheeler Park adjacent to the circus tents. Their fooling around left Irene covered in dirt and, knowing her parents would question it, rather than tell a more simple and inconsequential truth, James settled on a horrific lie: that she had been raped.

Now, it can't be certain the offense needed to be more severe than a supposed whistle to start this violence against innocent Black men because this hunger for revenge seemed to be brimming in Duluth for a long time. A reason to lynch was something just the right number of white citizens had been waiting for.

After the report of rape, the circus, which had already packed up and was on its way out of town, was stopped. About forty Black men were forced off the train and, out of them, fourteen taken into custody. Seven were released after questioning, and six remained: Elias Clayton, Elmer Jackson, Nate Green, Loney Williams, John Thomas, and Isaac McGhie. Isaac was the only one chosen to be a material witness, as opposed to being accused of rape. All of the men had gone from deplorable conditions in the circus to being in the hot seat for a crime they did not commit, but for white folk, this crime was easy to believe. None were identifiable to either Irene or James, but in the police chief's eyes something was "off" about their testimonies, which led to them still being held. The chief and a few others agreed to drive up to Virginia, Minnesota, to make more arrests from the circus train, not satisfied with the six men they had in custody.

Meanwhile, Irene was inspected by a doctor for physical evidence of the assault. Ultimately, the doctor concluded it probably wasn't rape due to nothing unusual about her exam.

William Henry was working the ore docks that fateful night, just outside of downtown on the bayfront. He worked overnight cleaning and watching over the ore and the ships. He had heard there was some commotion the night before regarding the rape of some girl at the circus at Wheeler Park by some Black men. He instantly flashed back to the horrors of Black men in the South being wrongly accused of looking at white women, whistling at white women, and, of course, raping white women—and the consequential actions often ending in their death.

Monday, June 15th, 1920 - 7:00 p.m.

```
How could this be happening here in Duluth!?
I just got into work and my white co-worker
tells me that several "niggers" raped a white
girl named Irene Tusken yesterday at the
circus. The rape was reported by her
boyfriend, the son of the owner of the
```

```
company that I work for. My co-worker
continued and said they rounded up all
Negro roustabouts earlier in the morning
from the circus train headed north. Worse
white men were talking about having a neck-
tie party. I can feel the tension building in
the City. I work the graveyard shift and
won't be off until morning. I need to get help
for these men as soon as possible. I pray for
their safety.
```

-William Henry

The Riot

    William Henry's prayers couldn't mean less to those who were out for blood. Once word got out that Irene had been raped, crowds rallied outside the police station doors where the six men were held. While the police chiefs were out making more arrests of Black circus workers, groups of white men demanded "justice" through strung necks. They rallied like bloodthirsty dogs waiting to pounce. The policemen left in the station were willing to fight them off at first, as their duties demanded, using a water hose to keep the rioters away from the windows they threatened to break. This wasn't as effective as the police had hoped because they were soon overtaken and the hose used against them. The station filled with water after one of the rioters blasted water through the windows. The heated crowd hurled threats of lynching them, too, due to being "nigger lovers." At this point, the policemen had to decide if a white man's life was worth losing over the matter, and the answer they concluded was no.

    The police gave up holding the angry mob back, and before long the mob broke into the cells and dragged out three men: Elias Clayton, Elmer Jackson, and Isaac McGhie. An estimated ten thousand people, racist rioters mixed with privileged couples just returning from a night out at the theater, gathered on the streets.

The Lynching

All figures of authority felt a lynching would never happen up North. The North wasn't the South, so the police chief wouldn't have to worry about keeping a close eye on the jail to make sure nothing got out of hand. Despite receiving multiple tips that a lynching would happen and that a mob was forming outside the station, the police were sure it would amount to nothing. Only after bricks were thrown into the station windows, and policemen blasted with the water hose and threatened to be lynched themselves, was the gravity of the situation realized.

This act was not motivated by justice, as the mob was just fine lynching a man—Isaac McGhie—detained only as a witness. All the innocent men in their cells could do was wait and pray while listening to the angry jeers of the mob and the destruction of the station. They curled into themselves and heard their names replaced with nigger bouncing off the jail walls. Then came the banging of metal against metal. At that point, they may have known there was no one to save them. No effort to hide under bed cots or plead to God would be enough to stop the white men who had it out for them. Being in the North meant nothing, and being a Black man meant everything. Elias, Elmer, and Isaac were dragged out of their cells and beaten. The mob took them up a hill adjacent to the station and hung them on the telegraph post as if they couldn't hear the three men pleading for their lives and insisting on their innocence. Racism knows no distance in a country built on it.

Tuesday, June 15th, 1920 - 9:00 p.m.

I pray to God that the rumors are not true. The white citizens of Duluth lynched three Negro men tonight! I can see and hear the mob from the docks. My co-workers warn me about going home right now. They said that justice was served tonight and that I don't want to get in the way of that. Where is the mayor? Where are the police? This can't be true! I see more and more Negros coming down here at the docks and hiding. Word has it that white folks done went crazy. I called home and Inga hasn't heard about anything, but she hears a lot of noise coming from downtown. She said Oscar wasn't home. Thank God Ethel is in Moose Lake.

-William Henry

The Echo in Desolation: A State of Complete Emptiness

Wednesday, June 16th, 1920 - 12:00 p.m.

This morning my soul was deeply shaken as I experienced the most intense feeling I ever had. I had the worst feeling that I ever had. I walked home from the docks across the bay and onto Main Street and down to 2nd Avenue to stop by the police station to ensure these Negro men in jail had help coming. I knew I had to make some calls down to St. Paul and Minneapolis for help. I just had to find out what was going on. Some good whites told me that the rumors were true that three men were broken out of jail and lynched. Also that there were men in jail still. They had told me to get home quickly because the streets weren't safe and the national guard would be downtown to secure the streets soon. I had a somber walk home. The streets felt unholy to me. As a walked up the 2nd Avenue hill up to my home, there they were ... bodies all beaten, broken and bruised just lying in the street at the foot of the telegraph post like trash that's going to be collected soon. They finally cut these young men down. My blood boiled! I was angry. I knew I had to get home and get my rifle just in case these Klan members decided to spread their hate into my home and my community. Looks like the southern breeze of Negro terrorism made it up north.

-William Henry

Wednesday, June 16th, 1920 in Moose Lake

Today I went to the post office to pick up my mail as I always did after the limited train came in. However, on this day no one spoke to me. I thought it was queer because over the past year most people that I was familiar with always said good morning and the postmaster often would joke with me about the amount of mail I got personally. I had been on a trip across the country a year earlier and there was a lot of people writing me.

I didn't know what it was, but I went back to the office and my boss was on the phone with Duluth, and he swung around and he said, "There's terrible trouble in Duluth. They're calling out the National Guard." And I asked why and he said, "It's a race riot." And I couldn't imagine that because knowing the Negroes in Duluth they're not that militant sort. But then he said that they've lynched some Negroes. Well, I couldn't reach my folks by phone, so I went through that day and then I realized what it was, the animosity in Moose Lake. That the feeling of-their

```
reaction seemed to be that they would have
liked to have been in on the lynching party.
```
-Ethel

    The word in Minnesota seemed not to fully align. Some newspapers labeled the event a disgrace and a stain on the town of Duluth. Others stated the Negro men were just like dogs and the only reasonable thing to do was to "put them down."

    Despite the absence of proof against the lynched men, despite the strong indication that the story of assault was a fabrication, to the contrary, the press of the country gave a wilder and more prominent display of these statements. The press promoted the narrative that Black men had attacked a white girl beyond a reasonable doubt. It was this narrative that caused the bestiality and mobbism that rang through the streets of Duluth. There was no attempt on the part of the press to correct the viciously misleading impression that had gone forth to the country. The New York Times carried an article with a single statement indicating the Chief of Police John Murphy had proven at least one of the men innocent, the rest of the article was still laced with falsehoods and significant exaggerations about what had transpired. But one had to ask, had they been charged? They were just taken off the train and detained—but did not make it through the night.

Photo Warning.
A photo of the actual lynching that occurred in Duluth, Minnesota is on the following pages 52-53. This image may cause visceral responses within readers. Please skip these pages if this is a concern.

A photo was taken to commemorate the lynching and circulated as a postcard - June 15, 1920.

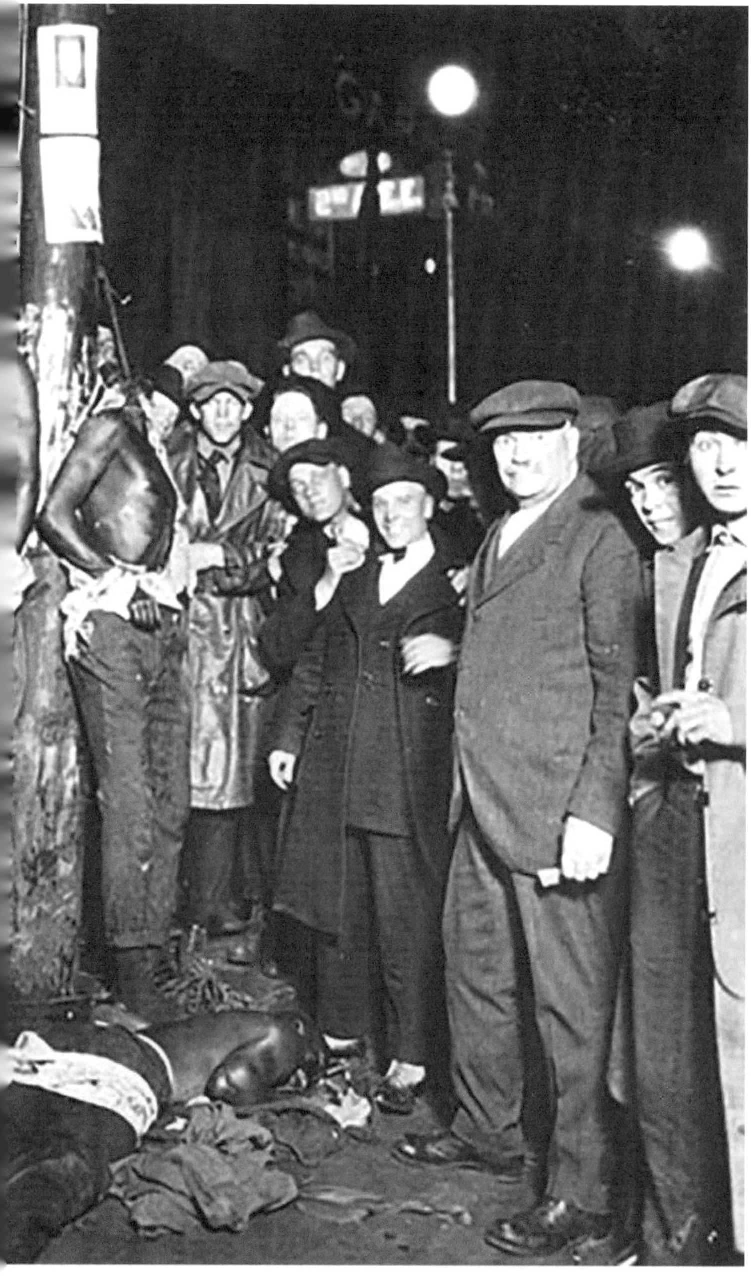

The Duluth Tragedy

The people of Duluth appear to express a greater amount of indignation over the lynching of three negroes in that city than they do over the terrible outrage that caused the stringing up of the black fiends. The city of Duluth is not disgraced. There have been lynchings in other cities and the towns survived the shock. Lynch law is to be deplored, but the crime which led up to the rule of the mob is more deplorable.

The city of Duluth can recover from any stigma that may be attached to the quick hanging of the negroes. A few years hence people will have forgotten the incident – but the unfortunate girl – what of her? She is the one to be considered. Her fate is far worse than that which has befallen the city.

. . .

"The Duluth Tragedy" by Editor
Mankato Daily Free Press
Mankato, Minnesota, June 17, 1920

THREE NEGROES HANGED BY MOB

Lynch Law Rules In Duluth and Attack On Young Girl is Avenged.

TROOPS RUSHED TO AID

5,000 Men Overpower Police, Break Down Cell Doors and Get Doomed Men—Lynch Law Court Preceeds Hanging.

St. Paul—Governor Burnquist announced that a thorough investigation of the Duluth lynching would be made.

"A searching investigation will be made. We will get to the bottom of it it is possible," he said. "I was pleased to learn that the St. Louis county attorney is arranging to present the case to a special grand jury without delay. Any cooperation that this office can give in the inquiry will be promptly forthcoming."

Duluth—Three negroes, attaches of a circus, arrested for attacking a 17-year-old white girl, were lynched in one of the city's main thoroughfares by a mob of 5,000 persons, which had stormed the police station with bricks and stones, and gained entry after overriding the city's police force.

"Three Negroes Hanged by Mob" by AP
Glenville Progress
Glenville, Minnesota, June 24, 1920

SATURDAY, JUNE 19, 1920

MINNESOTA'S DISGRACE.

The disgraceful carnal assault on a female and the disgraceful execution of mob vengeance on three men at Duluth, Minnesota, has been told so generally in the daily papers everywhere that no detailed account needs to be made by THE APPEAL.

But with the rest of the fair-minded papers and people we wish to add our condemnation of the crime of assault as perpetrated and also the murderous spirit of the mob. We cannot find words to express our utter horror of either or both, but will allow the sentiments expressed by others, with which we are in hearty accord, to in a measure do that for us.

The St. Paul Daily News said:

"That the three men were charged with the vilest of crimes is no justification for 'lynch law.' Had they been guilty, there is no doubt that proof, conviction and punishment would have followed swiftly—BUT—under due process of law.

"Minnesota's Disgrace" by Editor
T*he Appeal*
St. Paul, Minnesota, June 19, 1920

Duluth Appalled By Triple Tragedy

by Ray E. Austin
(Staff Representative Minneapolis Tribune)

Duluth, June 16. - Duluth has settled back to normal after a night and a day of revelry, for it was revelry that brought about the lynching of three negroes and set the city in mad turmoil. No one ever thought they would do it, was the way onlookers of the tragedy expressed it, for the crowd, it is said, was like people attending a carnival, giggling boys and girls looking skyward as though in wonderment at what hour the balloon would go up. All day long great crowds visited the scene of the lynching and the wrecked police station, where walls were battered in, windows smashed and cell bars cut into bits.

That there will be no further uprising or outbreak on the part of the lynchers is certain. The 10 negroes arrested at Virginia and placed in a hidding place on a farm near Vermillion road were escorted to Duluth this afternoon by companies of state troops and placed in the county jail.

...

"Duluth Appalled by Triple Tragedy" by Ray E. Austin
Minneapolis Tribune, Minneapolis, Minnesota, June 16, 1920.

The Black Grapevine

The "grapevine" was and is the formal and informal network among African Americans utilized to spread pertinent information the community needed.

" I thought there would be a lynching, but I still can't believe it happened."

" They didn't even try to be fair. The mob broke into the jail and stole three of them and lynched them."

" White people from all over Duluth were there. Everybody is a part of the KKK, the rich, the poor, men, women, children."

" The next night all the white people said they were going to run us out of town."

" After talking to the family and some neighbors, I think it's best if we just barricade ourselves at home for a few days. I'm getting my gun ready and anything else I can use to protect my family."

" Everybody is scared because of the lynching. So many left Duluth already. I hope Superior is safer for them."

" It's not safe to stay home. I'm hiding my family in the Bay. My neighbors went to Wisconsin. I know some families went all the way down to St. Paul."

" It's too dangerous to be on the streets. I don't think it's safe to even go out and get food."

BLACK KLANSMAN

when I watched the mob drag them by their feet,
I thanked God for passing me a white cloak

                                                    Get the nigger!
                                                  Get the nigger!
                                                  Get the nigger!

had I been born the color of
the caked mud in the circus tent,
I would have been dragged too

                                                    Get the nigger!
                                                  Get the nigger!
                                                  Get the nigger!

so I raised my fist with vigor
and let their echoes build in
my stomach and
exit my throat, raw with desperation

                                                    Get the nigger!
                                                  Get the nigger!
                                                  Get the nigger!

then it echoed up the hill
to the home where my mother lay her head
unsure if I was one of the niggers
who was sure to be dead.

                                                    Get the nigger!
                                                  Get the nigger!
                                                  Get the nigger!

but I ain't Ora and I'd be damned
if I die because a man spotted a nigger
who dared trying to stay alive.

                                                    Get the nigger!
                                                  Get the nigger!
                                                  Get the nigger!

when a familiar man caught me
betraying my black kin,
I ran up that hill ashamed
that I had the audacity to play pretend.

                                                    Get the nigger!
                                                  Get the nigger!
                                                  Get the nigger!

A Witness

It was said that Ethel's brother Oscar witnessed the riot firsthand, but his first instinct wasn't to run. He had been locking up the shoe shop where he worked after taking a nap in the store and was pushed by the momentum of the crowd to the corner of Second Avenue and Superior Street. The crowd was chanting, "Get the niggers! Get the niggers!" Oscar grew confused, not knowing what "niggers" the white folks were out for, considering so few of them resided there. It didn't take long for him to realize the crowd was a mob dragging Black men to the corner of First Street and Second Avenue East. The Black men were bloodied, stripped to the waist, beaten to a pulp, strung up the telegraph post, and lynched to the cheers of the crowd. The scene aroused anger inside Oscar's belly. A beast had been dormant deep within him his entire life. Without hesitation, he joined the chorus: "Lynch him! Lynch him!" His light skin and the dark sky allowed him to blend into the crowd, and he felt power not being the Black man in the spotlight. It didn't matter that he didn't know why it was happening; he didn't care to know because he felt safe—until he recognized the voice of a known KKK member by the name of Adolph Juten. The two of them had gone to school together, and Adolph knew what Oscar's blood was truly made of. They met eyes, and Oscar knew if he didn't make a quick escape, he'd be added to the bodies strung from the post. That was when Oscar ran up the hill and didn't dare look back.

Thursday, June 17th, 1920 in Moose Lake

I finally got a hold of my father. He was furious about the lynching—of course he was very upset, particularly because it was happening about four blocks from our home, outside the Shrine Temple, and as he walked home from work that next morning and up the hill back home the bodies had been cut down and were still lying there at the foot of this telegraph post.

Apparently fourteen Negroes that worked for the circus while it was in Duluth Monday were taken off a train. They said a white girl claimed that she had been raped by three Negroes while they were loading the train with all the circus paraphernalia late that night. She said that it was too dark to see those who raped her and that she only heard their voices. Well based on that I guess they locked up six of the Negro workers.

I also heard that they got their necktie party up by parading up and down the main street, and no one stopped them. No one seemed to . . . The Chief of Police was out of town; the mayor was out of town. Negro folk in downtown Duluth that day and night were scared for their lives. My father said when he got home that morning that he was ready for anyone that wasn't his family to come through that front door. I knew what he meant because he has rifles and shotgun always at the ready. And he knew how to use them because he went hunting all the time.

I know my father had a lot of remorse that he couldn't do anything about it . . . I don't think he believed it could happen up north and especially in Duluth. On all his trips down south and east, he would tell young people to come to Minnesota for a better life and that nothing was as bad as the south up north. Well he was wrong and I think he felt betrayed in a way by the hearts and souls of white folks in Duluth . . .

-Ethel

Lost in the Echo

None of the Ray family members were together when the lynching transpired. They were all left to process the news separately. When Oscar returned home from what seemed like a nightmare right outside the door of his home, he didn't utter a word. William Henry didn't bother to say a word either. They let the violence speak for itself and avoided direct eye contact with the only white person they could tolerate in the midst of the event. Inga didn't find out what had happened until Ethel returned home from Moose Lake a couple of days later. Even then, Ethel only spoke of her feelings about it with her father. Inga was left to think the avoidance meant her family looked at her as the enemy. She was the embodiment of what had caused those young men to die at the hands of a mob. A white woman whose words could flip a Black man's life upside down in an instant. Perhaps for being just that she was guilty, but she pushed back the thought and tried her best to support her family.

William Henry convinced himself he should have done more to help the young Black men, but his absence the night of the lynching was a blessing for his children because they knew that would have only ended in ruin. He was a proud man, unapologetic about his Blackness, and wouldn't be complacent with laying low to avoid stirring up trouble. He had the spirit of a Southern Black man unafraid to fight for his life.

Ethel's brother Will, on the other hand, lived out of state in Portland, Oregon when it all transpired. Ethel sent him a message with the news, and when he offered to come back, she told him it would be nothing but trouble. It was in his best interest as a Black man to stay away. Maybe it that moment when Will realized he could never live the lie if he ever went back to Duluth. He would be stuck with that fear of danger and immobilized. The only way to escape it was to never come back.

Aftermath

Thursday, June 17th, 1920

Mr. J. Louis Ervin, a fellow Negro Duluthian now a member of the St. Paul NAACP is up here trying to investigate what is going on. The NAACP and other organizations want all the perpetrators that broke out Elias Clayton, Elmer Jackson, and Isaac McGhie from jail tried for murder. In addition, they want every single person that touched, dragged, and hung them tried for murder. Judge William Cant is conducting a grand jury for this horrific crime. I don't know if the police, investigators, or prosecutors are up for charging their friends and relatives. May justice prevail!

-William Henry

Wednesday, June 30th, 1920

It's been several days now and things have cooled down around the City. While Ethel and I were on our trip touring the south a few months ago, we heard about a lynching in North Carolina. Now in my northern refuge there were three Negro circus hands that were hung. I was naive to believe that we were safe from such brutal acts. The Southern newspapers headlined this lynching occurring in the "free North." I've contacted Reverend William Majors of St. Mark's AME Church to discuss what needed to be done to get justice for these young men. I told him that now is the time to start the

Duluth Branch of the NAACP. Reverend Majors offered his church up as meeting space for our new organization. He told me that St. Mark's church and resources are committed to indict the lynchers. Many Black Duluthians planned to move out of Duluth as soon as possible. Ethel and I will be going to St. Paul to connect and get guidance from the St. Paul Branch of the NAACP on how to organize our branch up here.

-William Henry

Thursday, July 15th, 1920

Do you believe these white folks up here!? The grand jury just indicted seven more Negro men for the rape of that white girl! The NAACP just sent up three Negro lawyers- Frederick Barnett Jr., Charles W. Scrutchin, and R. C. McCullough. May God help them protect these men from further discrimination. White hate is thick in Duluth...

The grand jury is out and they issued thirty-seven indictments for the white people responsible for the death of Clayton, Jackson, and McGhie. However, they only charged twenty-five for rioting and twelve for murder. How is this possible! There were thousands out there that night and all who saw are minimally accomplices to murder!

-William Henry

Tuesday, August 10th, 1920

Thank God five of the Negro men's charges were dismissed, however, the other two Negros Max Mason and William Miller will be tried for the rape of Irene Tusken.

-William Henry

Friday, September 3rd, 1920

What a travesty of justice. Out of thirty-seven indictments only eight whites are going to be tried in court...

Thank God William Miller was acquitted of all charges. Godspeed to our brother, Max Mason. He was convicted of the rape of Irene and sentenced to seven to thirty years in prison! This is unbelievable! This is a lynching by trial! Is there no justice for the Negro?

Whites around Duluth are now feeling some sick vindication over Max's conviction as if they knew someone was guilty of the fabricated story. As if now the lynching of Elias Clayton, Elmer Jackson, and Isaac McGhie was justified and that the thousands that lynched them are now absolved of the deed.

-William Henry

Friday, September 17th, 1920

The St. Paul NAACP has reported that four white murderers were acquitted and one trial ended in a hung jury. Only three whites were tried for rioting-Louis Dondino, Carl Hammerberg, and Gilbert Stephenson. No one was convicted for murder! I have serious doubts about the justice system up here. I don't think any of those men guilty of simply rioting will serve anytime...

We officially started our Duluth Chapter of the NAACP. We have sixty-nine members! I was elected interim President until our first convention. We have much work to do.

-William Henry

4

Severance

Throughout high school, Ethel's brother Will had worked various jobs. In 1907, he was a driver for Cox Brothers Provision Co.; in 1908, he was a mailer at the Evening Herald newspaper; and in 1910, he worked as a clerk. But Will knew if he stayed in Duluth he would never be anything but the son of a Black man. To make something of his life, he felt he had to go as far away as possible from anything or anyone that chained him to that painful lineage, and ultimately pass as a white man.

During high school, Will found a novel published in 1900 in his father's library written by Charles W. Chesnutt. The book, The House Behind the Cedars, is about siblings John and Rena Warwick. John leaves their childhood home of Patesville, North Carolina, after the Civil War to start a new life in South Carolina passing as a white man. John and Rena are light skinned, born from mixed ancestry, their mother Black and their father white. John becomes a successful lawyer, marries a white woman, and has a son, Albert. However, John's wife dies, leaving him to raise their son by himself. John goes back home to North Carolina and asks his sister, Rena, to come to South Carolina to help him raise Albert.

Rena agrees to go with John to South Carolina, where she meets a white man named George Tryon, a business associate of her brother. George, who has no idea Rena is actually Black, falls in love with her, and they agree to marry.

Rena has serious anxiety about her Blackness being discovered by her fiancé and the white socialite community of which she is now a part. Rena becomes consumed by vivid dreams of evading and eluding her fiancé, who continues to find cultural clues of her true identity. One day, he finds out the truth and refuses to marry her. His discovery leads to both Rena and John being revealed. John tries to convince Rena that they both can move away and start over being white again and live the American dream once more.

From the novel, Will understood the risk he was taking in hopes of enjoying prosperity as a white man for however long he could. It was impossible if he stayed in Duluth.

Will wanted to travel and see other parts of the country. Working on the railroad gave him a sense of camaraderie and community among his fellow railroad workers. He found this shared purpose deeply rewarding because he yearned for social connection and a sense of belonging. When Will entered the railroad industry, he found a wide range of job opportunities with varying levels of skill and experience required. By 1909, the Northern Pacific Railroad was a major employer in Portland, Oregon, and had several different job opportunities, such as train conductor, locomotive engineer, brakeman, freight handler, station agent, and telegraph operator. Will had saved up enough money to buy a ticket to Portland on the Northern Pacific. Leaving home at the age of eighteen, he moved into a room in the rear of 355 Flanders while working as a waiter in Portland.

Marital Cloaks

Portland, Oregon, became Will's home base, and he worked on the railroad and as a waiter for several years. By age twenty-three, Will was a concrete worker in Pendleton, Oregon, when he met a stunningly beautiful woman, Mary Welch, who was thirty-eight years old but looked much younger.

She had gorgeous olive skin and confided in him that she was Colored. He admitted he was Colored as well, and they united as one. Mary told him she had been married twice before, once divorced, once widowed, with no children, and was also living in Pendleton. After a short courtship, they married in 1912 in Vancouver, Washington. World War I began in 1914, and Will chose not to enlist because he wanted to stay in Oregon to protect his wife. However, he knew something was wrong when Mary began disappearing for days and reappearing without explanation.

Initially, he worried that, being a Colored woman passing as white, she had been discovered by her employer and was being blackmailed to perform horrendous acts in exchange for keeping her identity a secret. Will refused to believe Mary was having an affair. But when Mary suggested Will enlist in the 1917–1918 draft, in exchange for honoring her request, he took the opening in communication to inquire about her frequent disappearances, and she revealed the sordid story that was her life.

The person he knew as Mary Welch was born Mary Smith in 1871, not 1874. Mary pulled out a box filled with documents and handed them to him one by one: adoption papers, marriage certificates, birth certificates, identification cards in several different names—one of which was verification that Mary was Native American, not Black, and had been living on an Indian reservation when they met.

When Will asked Mary if she was still married to someone else, she acted insulted, gathered her papers, packed her things, and left without uttering another word. He never heard from her again. He was shattered to learn that she was not Colored, that she was "Indian" and that she was receiving tribal compensation during their entire marriage.

Saturday, October 13th, 1917

```
The first World War was in progress and the
draft had begun. Will was eighteen when he
left home, and I was eight. As the older
brother he had been my protector in
"skirmishes" outside and with my brother,
Oscar. Will enlisted in the military while in
Duluth. He secured employment at the
shipyard and spent several months here
until his call to service came. It was a
wonderful reunion for me. We had long talks
```

about my desire to leave Duluth. He cautioned me about hastiness, and finally secured my promise to wait until he returned from service, and that then possibly we could work out something together. Will returned to the West Coast and reported for induction. I took continuous civil service examinations for stenographer, and always marked the blanks as to preferred location "would accept employment anywhere." I can't wait for the day he helps me leave Duluth.

-Ethel

Will's first marriage falling through didn't stop him from ultimately marrying to conceal his Black identity again. He married a white woman, Amanda Murphy, in Portland after the Duluth lynchings. She was divorced with a son fathered by a white man. They married in 1923, and he cloaked himself in the "white" protection his wife and stepson afforded him.

Wednesday, May 9th, 1923

Will promised after his service to help me leave Duluth. Yet here we are years later with Will constantly dodging my requests to move out west with him. Instead, he rather start a whole new life with a wife and son and forget about the family he already has.

-Ethel

To Die and Abandon

My brothers told me it ain't worth living like this.
It ain't worth the way their hearts race in fear.
They told me it was like death all over again.

They'd rather keep the W in the census.
Look at my mother. Look at my mother.
Write down that W in the census.

And I asked them what if they was with me?
And instead of telling me it ain't worth it
They married into white and forgot my name.

They'd rather keep the W in the census.
Look at my wife. Look at my wife.
Write down that W in the census.

But they didn't realize they still chose death
Told me the life of a Black man ain't worth it
And I asked "what about me?" and they laughed.

They'd rather keep the W in the census.
We want a life. We want a life.
Write down that W in the census.

Until they cried and said, "it ain't worth it."
I wonder if they still felt their heart race
When a white man stared at them too long.

There's a W in the census.
Look at my skin. Look here within.
There's a W in the census.

But it ain't worth it.
It ain't worth it.
It ain't worth it.

What Does the Census Say?

The last column on the right is "Race." The Census pattern of William Henry's "Race" is ever evolving. He self-designated as "white" or "mulatto" up until 1920. After the lynching in Duluth, William Henry designated himself as "Negro" or "Black" from 1930 until his death.

1900 Census: William Henry, Inga, Will and Ora are listed as "W" for white.

1910 Census: William Henry, Oscar, and Ethel are listed as "Mu" for mulatto. Inga is "W" for white.

1920 Census: William Henry, Inga, Ethel, and Oscar are listed as "W" for white.

1930 Census: William Henry and Catherine Shrewsburg (lodger) are listed as "Neg" for Negro/Black. Inga is listed as "W" for white.

A Privilege for a Life

Oscar and Will insisted that "being white" was the only acceptable way to live. If they could pass, they thought it foolish not to play the role. It can't be certain whether their reasoning was solely for safety. Oscar went on to discriminate against any Black folk who wanted to work at the store he ran later in life. Possibly he feared the mere sight of one could cause customers to see similar features. Maybe, he thought they would discover Oscar was a nigger like them and his throat would be next. How or if Oscar had a relationship with his father—the reason for his mixed heritage and living proof that he had more than one drop in him—is a wonder. He paid his dues for the privilege by driving the nigger out of himself and every space he inhabited.

All Will left behind for his Black family were traces of letters, perhaps some genuine worry, but above all he never looked back. The man found peace hiding behind his new white family and couldn't have been more content. In a way, both men followed in their father's footsteps. They ran for some semblance of freedom. They ran to gain more opportunities than their place (social or physical) could afford. Yet, in Black eyes, their deeds may have brought more shame than pride. We are left asking what sacrifices are excusable for the sake of survival.

Ethel, the proud Black woman, faced those fears. Amongst all of the worlds presented to her (Black, white, mixed, Ethel), she settled most comfortably into the Black identity. Understandably, she may have been in a better position to do so because of the higher appetite for Black men when it came to lynching. Ethel, however, was proudly Black. Her activism and bravery towered over her brothers' fears, and she proved to be a woman of great substance.

Ethel Ray, circa 1920

The Neophyte

After the lynchings that occurred in Duluth, William Henry and Ethel knew the Negro community needed assurance they could safely remain without further threat of unprovoked violence. Klan activity in Minnesota grew significantly the following year, 1921. Just one year after the lynchings, Klan recruiting reached north from its Georgia headquarters to Duluth. A Chicago member joined the members from Minneapolis to help organize the Duluth Klan chapter. The Duluth Herald stated in August 1921:

The great majority of the individuals in the Klan are men of good intentions, although narrow and without much vision. They fail to grasp the essentials of American history. They do not know that one of the big things our ancestors fought for was doing away with autocratic power, exercised by irresponsible tribunals, lawless or even, in the old days, lawful. When these persons see this, the Ku Klux Klan will be reformed from within . . . It would be shocking if a majority of the people in the Klan were bad citizens. They are not. In fact, they fairly represent public opinion in the places where they flourish. One year later, the Klan claimed that the Duluth-area chapter had 1,500 members. Six Ku Klux Klan representatives also arrived in Minneapolis in 1921, and in August, North Star Klan No. 2 began holding meetings at Olivet Methodist Church on East Twenty-Sixth Street and at Foss Memorial Church at the corner of Fremont and Eighteenth Avenue North. While chapters in Minneapolis and St. Paul probably attracted the most members, people from Cass Lake and Walker in the north to Austin, Albert Lea, and Owatonna in the south began flocking to KKK rallies, meetings, and picnics.

```
Friday, March 4th, 1921
I've been working fervently between Duluth
and the Twin Cities to make our NAACP
chapter as efficient and impactful as
possible. It is a lot of work but it is worth
it. Since our Duluth chapter is new, we still
need resources and guidance on the best way
```

> to run it. I know W. E. B. Du Bois will be in
> the Twin Cities next month. My dad wants me
> to help convince him to come up to Duluth
> with me. Having Du Bois speak up north would
> gather support and attention to the
> injustice of lynchings and hopefully gain
> more support to pass the Anti-Lynching law
> in Minnesota.
>
> -Ethel

The Appeal, a Negro newspaper from St. Paul and Minneapolis, stated that Du Bois had been in the Twin Cities to speak on the Pan-African Congress, though the local NAACP community wanted him there to help fight to get the Dyer Anti-Lynching legislation passed. This bill, proposed in 1918 by Missouri state representative Leonidas Dyer, would make lynching a federal felony punishable by imprisonment. Convincing Du Bois to come to speak in a little town that had recently made headlines for its large-scale lynching was a hard bargain. But after some coaxing, he agreed and Ethel accompanied him the 150 miles to Duluth the morning after his talk in Minneapolis at the People's Church. The man whom she had watched everyone, including her father, put on a pedestal became someone just like her. What was special about him was his ability to speak up and speak clearly. Du Bois was a man who could get his point across and navigated his spaces with humility. On March 21, 1921, Ethel Ray introduced W.E.B. Du Bois at St. Marks AME Church:

> Good evening, ladies and gentlemen, I wish to pay special tribute to the splendid cooperation of the St Paul and Minneapolis NAACP Branches in raising money for lawyers, reporters, and investigators of the Duluth lynching.

I found a poem with which I have concluded …

Men perish, but their power goes on forever
As time goes on, we find that there is a deliverer
Bequeathed to every just cause.

Great Lincoln, now with glory graced
All god-like with the pen
Our chattel fetters broke
And placed us in the ranks of men.

But even he could not awake the dead
Nor make alive,
Nor change stern Nature's laws,
Which makes the fitted to survive.

Though wrongs there are,
And wrongs have been,
And wrongs we still must face
We have more friends than foes
Within the Anglo-Saxon race.

In spite of all the Babel cries
Of those who rage and shout,
God's silent forces daily rise
To bring His will about.

Our portion is, and yet will be
To drink a bitter cup
In many things, yet all must see,
The race is moving up.

Ladies and Gentlemen, look to the east from whence cometh all light; otherwise, darkness is intense. I take pleasure in introducing to you the rising sun, Dr. W. E. B. Du Bois.

Monday, March 21st, 1921

What a turn out! W. E. B. Du Bois came all the way up to Duluth and captivated everyone. He spoke at the St. Marks AME Church. The church is only supposed to have 250 people in it, but I know we far exceeded that limit. It wasn't just Black people in the crowd either, probably about three-fourths of the audience was white. I just know Du Bois being the very first speaker for our chapter foreshadows us doing great things!

-Ethel

The meeting was held at the Black church, St. Mark's on Fifth Avenue, and it was a decided success with more than three hundred people present, the greater portion of whom were white. They secured sixty new NAACP members and split the collection three ways: to the church to pay interest on its mortgage, to the national NAACP office, and the balance to their local NAACP treasury. This event may have been the start of Ethel's journey into unabashed activism. However, the NAACP wasn't the only organization to grow.

The KKK in Minnesota

Shortly after the Duluth lynchings, Minnesota became the first state to pass an anti-lynching law, in 1922. Ironically, the Ku Klux Klan gained momentum, holding its first documented meeting in Minnesota. The following year approximately ten Klan chapters were reported to be active in Minneapolis alone. Many chapters appeared on college campuses throughout the Midwest, and nationally, leading to the Klan's membership swelling to over one hundred thousand.

By 1923, George Leach, the Minneapolis mayor launched an investigation into possible Klan activity at the University of Minnesota. The school paper, the Minnesota Daily, reported suspected student Klan members. That same year, the Klan failed in their attempt to ruin the reelection of Mayor Leach. Two years later, the KKK received their certificate of incorporation, sanctioned by the State, for their non-profit organization.

Leaving for a New Opportunity

Sunday, September 3rd, 1922

Duluth and Moose Lake couldn't hold me anymore. I felt I was prepared for a greater vocation in life. Working at the Minnesota Forest Fire Relief Commission paid well enough. I have been there for a few years. It's time to move on though. Mrs. Nellie Francis, a surrogate mother of mine, encouraged me to apply as a Legislative Clerk at the State capital. I will do that. This move will be a great change of scenery for me. I met so many people in St. Paul and Minneapolis. I love the supportive community down there and I found myself visiting my friends for weeks at a time.

-Ethel

Wednesday, October 4th, 1922

I went to the post office today. I'm so excited. I have received the letter from the Minnesota Legislature. I got the position! I will be the first Colored woman to have that position. I will get paid $6 a week as a stenographer and typist. I will serve on three committees- Education, Apportionment, and Bank and Banking. My employment term is only for five months January 1923 through May 1923. I will be looking for other opportunities elsewhere. I really want to work with a civic or social agency that serves my community.

-Ethel

Colored Girl Is Appointed Clerk In Legislature

Miss Ethel M. Ray of Duluth, daughter of Mr. and Mrs. W. H. Ray of Duluth, has been selected as one of the committee clerks in the legislature. Miss Ray is an efficient stenographer and typist, having served as stenographer two years during the settlement of the Moose Lake fire claims.

She was rated 100% for efficiency and courtesy upon inspection and has been assigned to three important committees. Several requests were made for her services. Miss Ray is an attractive young lady of very refined manners and a credit to her race.

Wednesday, December 13, 1922, *The Appeal*

Epilogue

In January 1923, Ethel left her Duluth hometown for the city of St. Paul. After five months clerking at the Minnesota State Capitol, she did go on to work with civic and social agencies that served her Black community across the country—in Kansas City, Chicago, New York, Seattle, and San Fransisco, where she ended up living from 1944 until her death in 1992, at the age of ninety-three. During those years, her contributions included, among many others, being Minneapolis's first Black policewoman, administrative assistant with the NAACP, and secretary to W. E. B. Du Bois at the founding of the United Nations.

As for Ethel's family, William Henry Ray was done hiding too. He stopped having Inga tell the census collectors to put a "W" by his name and instead put a "Neg" for Negro. The false concept of "race" negatively impacted all of their children's identities, leading them to feel the need to choose one or the other. William Henry and Inga's children just could not be who they were, African-Swedish American citizens trying to make their way through life like everyone else. The myth of "race" and the painful practice of racism caused the Ray family to learn different ways to navigate in all the worlds they existed in.

Ethel was mentored into her identity by the Black communities in Duluth, St. Paul, and Minneapolis but, most importantly, by her Black father. Her Blackness was not about race; it was about the human existence of a people. Indeed, her vocation was ever transforming and led her to address the social injustices of her time. She was forever changed by her pilgrimage with her father across the county and by the lynchings of Elias Clayton, Elmer Jackson, and Isaac McGhie all the way up in the North.

Black newspapers throughout the country mentioned Ethel's accomplishments whenever they got the chance, because she was exceptional and Black. More importantly, it was expected that those with notable skills return to and serve the people who nurtured them and their community, and indeed, Ethel did this.

Ethel Ray made it through what must have felt like a "rites of passage." Being "mixed race" in America during the early 1900s meant no escaping the multiple worlds that defined her—trying to find a place in the white, existing in the gray, and living in the black. Ethel learned she had the power to choose her reality. She chose to be Black.

Acknowledgments

I would like to express my heartfelt gratitude to the following individuals who have played a crucial role in the creation of this book:

Rekhet Si-Asar, In Black Ink executive director, for her invaluable guidance and support throughout this entire process.

Anura Si-Asar, In Black Ink managing editor, for his tireless efforts in assisting with various aspects of this project.

In Black Ink editors, Uri-Biia Si-Asar and Lenny Prater, for their meticulous attention to detail and their invaluable contributions in refining the manuscript.

Daniel Oyinloye and Henry Banks for their understanding of the significant contributions made by Ethel Ray, as well as continually supporting me in my pursuit to tell my grandmother's story.

Michael Fedo for his groundbreaking work, *The Lynchings in Duluth* (1976), which shed light on the atrocities committed against three innocent Black men: Elias Clayton, Elmer Jackson, and Isaac McGhie.

Danielle Magnuson for her meticulous copyediting. Danielle's keen eye for detail and commitment to precision have ensured this book is polished and error-free. Her dedication to maintaining the highest standards of quality is deeply appreciated.

Christopher Harrison for his exceptional talent and creativity as the book designer. His artistic vision and skillful execution have resulted in a visually stunning and captivating book. His ability to bring the words to life through design is truly remarkable, and I am grateful for the beauty and professionalism Christopher brought to this project.

Smith Printing Company LLC for their exceptional printing services. Their commitment to excellence and attention to detail have ensured this book is of the highest quality. I am grateful for their dedication to delivering a product that exceeds expectations.

Leslie Barlow for the captivating cover design. Her artistic prowess and ability to capture the essence of this book in a single image have resulted in a cover that is both visually striking and thematically resonant. Leslie's creativity and talent have made a lasting impression.

To all those mentioned above, your contributions have been pivotal in shaping this book into what it is today. I am deeply grateful for your expertise, dedication, and unwavering support. Thank you for being an integral part of this journey and for helping bring this book to fruition.

Appendix

Timeline

Family Tree

The Black Population in Minnesota

List of Images

List of Poems

References and Resources

About the Author

Timeline

1861
US Civil War begins (April 12)

1865
US Civil War ends (April 9)

Ku Klux Klan founded in Pulaski, Tennessee (December 24)

Reconstruction occurs (1865–1877)

1868
William Henry Ray born in Oberlin, North Carolina, now known as Raleigh, North Carolina.

1870
Inga Nordquist born in Eksharad, Varmland County, Sweden.

1872
Henry Ray (William Henry's father) dies. William Henry is four years old.

1877
Reconstruction ends and federal troops withdraw from South.

1878
William Henry leaves North Carolina. He is ten years old.

1879
William Henry arrives in Davenport, Iowa. He is eleven years old.

1888
Inga immigrates to United States and begins working at Ardmore Hotel in Minneapolis. She is seventeen years old.

William Henry begins working at Ardmore Hotel (August 23). He is twenty years old.

1889
Courtship between William Henry and Inga begins (March 7)

Inga leaves Ardmore Hotel and begins work as a domestic (May 3)

William Henry leaves Ardmore Hotel and begins work on the railroad (June)

Inga is pregnant (October)

1890

William Henry and Inga move to Duluth and rent a house (February 6)

William Henry begins work at Spalding Hotel (February 7)

William Henry and Inga marry (May 14)

William "Will" Nordquist Ray, their first child, born in Duluth (June 23)

Ray family moves to Two Harbors; William Henry and Inga work at a boardinghouse.

William Henry meets John Beargrease.

1893

Ora Inga Ray, their second child, born in Two Harbors (January)

1895

Oscar Edwin Ray, their third child, born in Two Harbors (January 25)

1898

Ray family moves back to Duluth and buys a home at 209 East 5th Street.

1899

Ethel May Ray, their fourth and last child, born in Duluth (April 13)

1900

Ora dies (October 1) of pneumonia. She was seven years old.

1905

Ethel attends kindergarten and first grade at Franklin Elementary (1905–1907)

1907

Franklin Elementary burns down; Ethel attends second through eighth grades at Nettleton Elementary (1907–1914).

1910

John Beargrease dies.

1914

World War I begins in Europe (June 28)

Ethel attends Duluth Central High (1914–1917)

Ethel takes civil service examinations for stenographer during high school.

1917

United States enters World War I (April 6)

Ethel graduates from Duluth Central High School (June 13)

1918

Ethel works as stenographer and investigator for Minnesota Forest Fire Relief Commission in Moose Lake, while also working as secretary for Charles Mahnke at the Moose Lake Star-Gazette (October 1918–March 1919).

World War I ends (November 11)

Ethel returns to Moose Lake to fill in for a sick colleague - Minnesota Forest Fire Relief Commission (December)

1919

Ethel works at Minnesota Forest Fire Relief Commission in Moose Lake (March 1919–August 1922).

Ethel travels with her father around the country on a four-month trip (December 1919–March 1920).

1920

A mob in Duluth lynches three Black men—Elias Clayton, Elmer Jackson, and Isaac McGhie (June 15). Ethel is twenty-one years old.

1921

NAACP founding member W. E. B. Du Bois speaks to the citizens of Duluth (March 21)

1922

Ethel returns to Duluth after three years working in Moose Lake.

1923

Ethel leaves Duluth for St. Paul and becomes Minnesota State Legislature's first African American stenographer (January–May).

Ethel works for Kansas City Urban League.

Ethel attends summer school in Chicago with National Playground Association.

1924

During Harlem Renaissance, Ethel works for Charles Johnson at National Urban League in New York City (May 1924–November 1925).

1926

Phyllis Wheatley House in Minneapolis hires Ethel as assistant head resident (March).

1928

Ethel becomes Minneapolis Police Department's first African American policewoman—and first African American policewoman in state. (April 1928–January 1931).

1929

Ethel marries LeRoy Alexis Herbert Williams in Anoka, Minnesota (August 3).

1933

Thatcher Popel Willliams, Ethel's first child, was born in Washington, D.C. (January 11).

During Ethel's pregnancy, she suffered a cataclysmic attack of acute arthritis that left her with a limp. This led her to quit the police department.

At this time her husband also lost his job, and accepted his family's offer to come to Maryland to live with them.

1934

Glenn Ray Williams, Ethel's second child, born in Duluth, Minnesota

Ethel serves as Assistant to Director of Unemployment Survey under ERA (Equal Rights Amendments).

1935

Ethel returns to Twin Cities to work for Minnesota Negro Council (January–April).

1937

Ethel works for Minnesota Department of Education (April 1937–September 1940).

1940

Ethel works for Hampton Institute in Virginia (1940–1943).

1943

Ethel and LeRoy divorce (February18)

1944

Ethel marries Clarence Aristotle Nance in Seattle (February 2).

Thatcher and Glenn, Ethel's sons, change their last name to Nance.

1945
Nance family moves to San Francisco, California.

Founding conference of the United Nations held in San Fransisco; Ethel works as secretary for W. E. B. Du Bois, who represents the NAACP as a consultant to American delegation (April 25–June 26).

Ethel serves as Special Administrative Assistant at NAACP Regional Office in San Francisco (1945–1955).

1948
William Henry Ray dies in San Francisco while visiting his daughter Ethel Ray Nance on November 27.

1949
Inga Nordquist Ray dies in Duluth. (January 19)

1951
Ethel becomes a member of California Bay Area NAACP–GI Assistance Committee.

1963
Oscar dies (July 8)

1970
Will Norquist dies (August 25)

1971
Ethel is a member of Advisory Committee of a joint project with Bancroft Library at University of California, Berkeley, and NAACP Regional Office on a Repository of Historical Documents.

1978
At seventy-nine years old, Ethel becomes oldest individual to receive a bachelor's degree from University of San Francisco.

1992
Ethel passes away at the age of ninety-three (July 11).

Family Tree

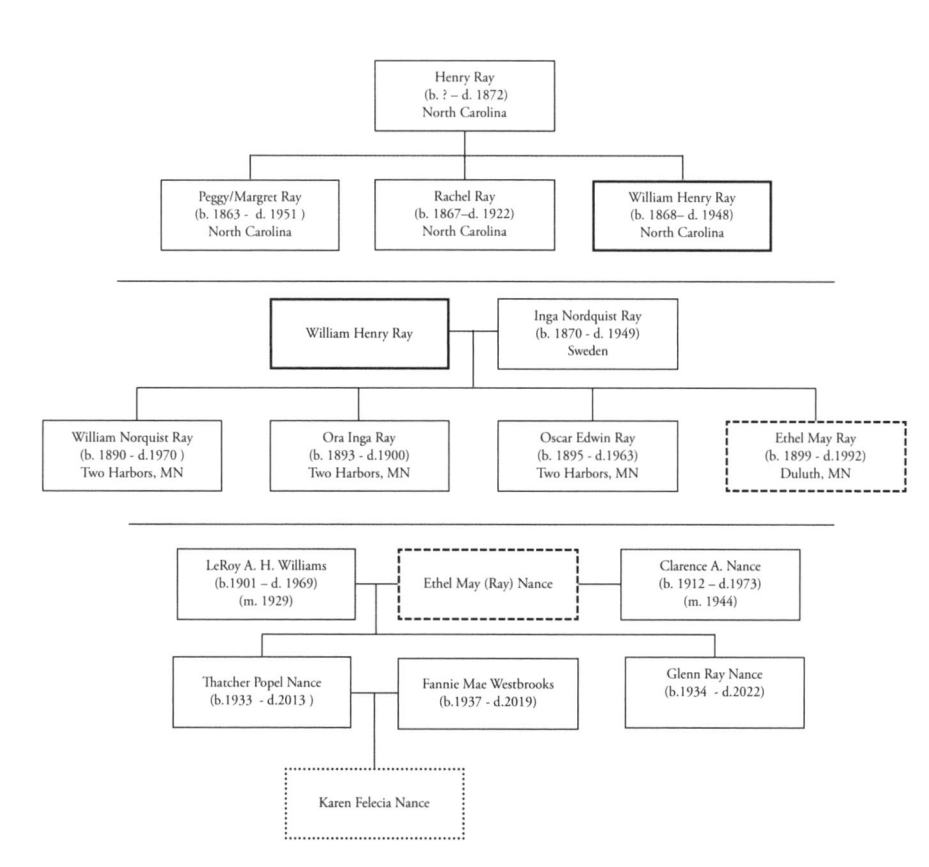

Henry Ray
(b. ? – d. 1872)
North Carolina

- **Peggy/Margret Ray** (b. 1863 - d. 1951) North Carolina
- **Rachel Ray** (b. 1867–d. 1922) North Carolina
- **William Henry Ray** (b. 1868– d. 1948) North Carolina

William Henry Ray — **Inga Nordquist Ray** (b. 1870 - d. 1949) Sweden

- **William Norquist Ray** (b. 1890 - d.1970) Two Harbors, MN
- **Ora Inga Ray** (b. 1893 - d.1900) Two Harbors, MN
- **Oscar Edwin Ray** (b. 1895 - d.1963) Two Harbors, MN
- **Ethel May Ray** (b. 1899 - d.1992) Duluth, MN

LeRoy A. H. Williams (b.1901 – d. 1969) (m. 1929) — **Ethel May (Ray) Nance** — **Clarence A. Nance** (b. 1912 – d.1973) (m. 1944)

- **Thatcher Popel Nance** (b.1933 - d.2013) — **Fannie Mae Westbrooks** (b.1937 - d.2019)
- **Glenn Ray Nance** (b.1934 - d.2022)

Karen Felecia Nance

The Black Population in Minnesota

The Black population in Minnesota has historically been small. According to the census in 1890, state's total population was 1,310,283 and the Black population was 3,683—only 0.3 percent. The state's Black population remained below 1 percent for many years but began growing significantly between 1950 and 1970, during the last phase of the Great Migration of African Americans from Southern states to the North, Midwest, and West. Although Minnesota's Black population did not increase as much as the populations of other Northern states such as Illinois and Michigan, during this twenty-year period, it rose by 149 percent. In 1980, the state's total population was 4,075,970 and its Black population was 53,344 (1.3 percent). By 2020, the census reported Minnesota's total population as 5,706,494 compared to the Black population of 398,494—about 7 percent of the total population. The second migration of Black people to Minnesota from 1990 to 2020 is due to the influx of diverse Black populations immigrating from Africa, particularly Somalia and Ethiopia, and the Caribbean. "Black" as a definition for census purposes is self-chosen. The data of the Black population reported here is not simply inclusive of African Americans who have been in the United States for twenty-five generations but, rather, includes multi-ethnicities and nationalities who see Black as their primary identity for counting purposes.

In the decade after the Duluth lynchings, between 1920 and 1930, the white population of Duluth increased by at least 2,000 people, and the city's Black population dropped from 495 to 416, a decrease of 16 percent. In fact, Black people didn't start repopulating Duluth until the 1950s, after at least a generation of erasure of the 1920 violence had occurred. The decrease in Duluth's Black population from 1920 to 1950 was 33 percent, or a third, of its Black community. However, from 1950 to 1960, there was a 40 percent increase of Black people living in Duluth.

Black Population in Minnesota 1890 - 2020

Year	Duluth	St. Paul	Minneapolis	Minnesota
1890	155	1,624	1,317	3,683
1900	264	2,263	1,616	4,959
1910	410	3,144	2,712	7,084
1920	495	3,376	3,806	8,809
1930	416	4,001	4,179	9,445
1940	309	4,139	4,431	9,928
1950	334	5,655	6,782	14,022
1960	555	8,240	11,589	22,263
1970	857	10,848	19,114	34,868
1980	742	13,242	28,564	53,344
1990	697	19,435	46,467	94,944
2000	1,390	33,637	67,966	171,731
2010	1,988	43,615	70,011	282,791
2020	1,988	51,402	81,262	398,494

Population in Minnesota 1890 - 2020

Year	Duluth	St. Paul	Minneapolis	Minnesota
1890	33,115	135,156	164,738	1,310,283
1900	52,969	163,065	202,718	1,751,394
1910	78,466	214,744	301,408	2,075,708
1920	98,917	234,698	380,582	2,387,125
1930	101,453	271,606	464,370	2,563,953
1940	101,065	287,736	521,718	2,792,300
1950	104,511	311,349	482,872	2,982,483
1960	107,312	313,411	434,400	3,413,864
1970	105,078	309,980	370,951	3,804,971
1980	92,811	270,230	368,383	4,075,970
1990	85,493	272,235	382,618	4,375,099
2000	86,918	287,151	382,578	4,919,479
2010	86,265	285,068	429,954	5,303,925
2020	86,697	311,527	425,336	5,706,494

US Census Bureau, census.gov
Census Decennial Publications for Minnesota, General Population Characteristics 1890–2020

List of Images

Photo of young William Henry Ray, circa 1880s   Page 5
Ethel Ray Nance Family Archive
Karen Felecia Nance, San Francisco, California

Photo of William Henry and Inga Ray, 1889   Page 8
Ethel Ray Nance Family Archive
Karen Felecia Nance, San Francisco, California

Will, Inga and Oscar after the Funeral of Ora, 1900   Page 15
(Photo by William Henry)
Ethel Ray Nance Family Archive
Karen Felecia Nance, San Francisco, California

Advertisement for John Robinson's Circus   Page 44
Duluth Herald, June 10, 1920, page 11.
From Minnesota Historical Society, MNOPEDIA
mnhs.org/sites/default/files/records/documents/00001835.pdf

African Dodger Game Flier   Page 45
Kelly, Erin. (2023). "The History of Racist Carnival Games Like 'African Dodger' —Which Evolved into the Dunk Tanks Still Used Today" allthatsinteresting.com/african-dodger

Lynching in Duluth, Minnesota postcard, 1920   Pages 52-53
Henry Banks/Duluth Lynching Memorial Archive
In Black Ink, St. Paul, Minnesota

Newspaper clippings regarding the Duluth lynchings   Pages 54-57

  "The Duluth Tragedy" by Editor
  Mankato Daily Free Press (Mankato, Minnesota), June 17,1920, page 6
  White owned

"Three Negroes Hanged by Mob" by AP
Glenville Progress (Glenville, Minnesota), June 24, 1920, page 2
White owned

"Minnesota's Disgrace" by Editor
The Appeal (St. Paul and Minneapolis, Minnesota), June 19, 1920, page 2.
Black owned

"Duluth Appalled by Triple Tragedy" by Ray E. Austin
Minneapolis Tribune (Minneapolis, Minnesota), June 17, 1920, page 1
White owned

US Census, William Henry Ray household   Page 72

1900 US Federal Census
Minnesota, St. Louis County, Duluth Ward 03, District 0267

1910 US Federal Census
Minnesota, St. Louis County, Duluth Ward 03, District 0165

1920 US Federal Census
Minnesota, St. Louis County, Duluth Ward 03, District 0112

1930 US Federal Census
Minnesota, St. Louis County, Duluth Ward 03, District 0057

Photo of Ethel Ray, circa 1920   Page 74
Ethel Ray Nance Family Archive
Karen Felecia Nance, San Francisco, California

"Colored girl is appointed clerk in legislature"   Page 80
The Appeal (St. Paul and Minneapolis, Minnesota), December 13, 1922.

List of Poems

Poems written by Lanise "Lenny" Prater

Before the Homeowners Association (HOA)	P. 12
Who Poisoned Me?	P. 16
Seed to Root	P. 32
Black Klansman	P. 59
To Die and Abandon	P. 71

About the Poet

Lenny Prater is a poet, activist, and young professional. In St. Paul, they started as a summer intern with In Black Ink after graduating from Macalester College and have continued working with IBI after moving to New York City to be surrounded by likeminded creatives. Lenny is passionate about sharing artistic forms of storytelling and practices it through their poetry, art, and programming.

References and Resources

Ethel Ray Nance Archive
San Francisco, California
Housed and owned by Karen Felecia Nance

Henry Banks/Duluth Lynching Memorial Archive
St. Paul, Minnesota
Housed at In Black Ink

"Nance, Ethel Ray (1899–1992)"
MNOPEDIA
mnopedia.org/person/nance-ethel-ray-1899-1992

St. Mark's African Methodist Episcopal Church
Duluth, Minnesota
stmark-ame.org/history

Fedo, Michael, The Lynchings in Duluth, Second edition
Minnesota Historical Society Press, St. Paul, Minnesota

The Appeal, St. Paul and Minneapolis, Minnesota 1920–1923
African American weekly newspaper, John Quincy Adams, editor

Ouse, David. "Ethel Ray Nance." Zenith City Online, February 13, 2014
Zenith City Press, Duluth, Minnesota
zenithcity.com/archive/people-biography/ethel-ray-nance

Minnesota Black History Project: Interview with Ethel Ray Nance
Oral History Collection, Minnesota Historical Society, St. Paul, Minnesota
Description: Mrs. Nance discusses her family background, the Duluth black community in the early 1900s, the 1920 lynchings in Duluth, the Moose Lake Fire Relief Commission (1918) and her work experiences. OH 43.16

Ethel Ray Nance Papers, 1895–1979
Manuscript Collection, Minnesota Historical Society, St. Paul, Minnesota
Description: Includes newspaper clippings, correspondence, and biographical information on Ethel Ray Nance. P1852

A Century-Old Injustice: Remembering the 1920 Duluth Lynchings
https://www.mnd.uscourts.gov/sites/mnd/files/Open-Doors-2021_Packet_of_Materials.pdf

Duluth Lynchings: Resources relating to the tragic events of June 15, 1920
Minnesota Historical Society, St. Paul, Minnesota
mnhs.org/duluthlynchings

Duluth moves to punish lynchers, T*he New York Times*, New York, New York. Thursday, June 17, 1920.

About the Author

Karen Felecia Nance, Esquire, is a multifaceted professional with extensive expertise as a mediator, attorney, author, private investigator, restorative justice facilitator, public speaker, and podcast host. She holds a BA degree from the University of California, Berkeley, and a JD from Temple University in Philadelphia, Pennsylvania. Throughout her career, Karen has excelled in various legal realms, including civil litigation, criminal defense, and prosecution, as well as child support, child custody, and child visitation.

In addition to her legal background, Karen has immersed herself in different cultures through her travels to East, West, and Central Africa, with plans to visit North and South Africa. Her passion for inclusivity extends beyond borders, as she has collaborated with international adoptees, and individuals with developmental disabilities.

Karen's law practice is centered around advocating for respect and amplifying the voices of all individuals, ensuring their perspectives are valued and heard.

Karen is the granddaughter of Ethel Ray Nance.

karennance.com